MY GIFT TO YOU

Holiday & Spice
Its Always Nice

T.K. RICHARDS

T.K. Richards 24

TK
RICHARDS

ISBN: 978-1-959253-24-2

First printing, 2023 LNK Publishing"

About This Work

This novel contains mature themes and is intended for a **Mature Audience**.

Content warnings include:
*Open door, detailed steamy scenes
*Profanity
*Mentions of alcohol
*Mentions of racial profiling

Tropes
Instalove
Rejected Mates
Secret Money
Second Chance
Grumpy/Sunshine
Pining Mates

Note From The Author

This book is a work of fiction and contains stories of historic roots lived in the southern hemisphere of The United States. Supporting characters in this work speak with Geechee/Gullah dialect, AAVE slang, and British slang. Some words are spelled to reflect the sound that represent their appropriate region, and how the character speaks. For example, **there** may be spelled as **they,** or **they** may be spelled as **dey**, and italicized for ease of recognition it is regional.

The characters in this book are featured in two separate series. To become familiar with their stories that take prior to the time period of this mashup, the reading order is featured on the following page.

READING ORDER

I have waited for this opportunity for more than half a century, to repeat to you once again my vow of eternal fidelity and everlasting love.

— Nelson Mandela

Chapter 1

Rockin' Around

Levi

THRUSTING BETWEEN HER WET WALLS ALL night has weakened me to no avail, but I'm wide awake, inhaling the lingering scent of peaches and faded mint on her skin. I hold Launa close in my arms, thinking of the proper way to apologize for being too rough last night.

She squirms and grunts in her sleep, searching for comfort on my chest to support her head. All feels right with the world with her lying next to me. I hope she feels the same.

This sharp, tingly feeling in my chest has turned me into a liar. I vowed never to give my all or my heart to another woman after the first Mrs. King burned me, but this connection Launa and I share surprises me. I kid myself, trying to play it down that I'm a man in love.

Overwhelmed by my ability to love again—and trust again—I feel foolish for falling so hard. So fast. But when I look at her, all I see is my second chance to get it right this time.

She wiggles once more as the conversation

I'm having in my head swells my chest with anxiety and fear. *Tell her she's more than a fling. More than a warm body to run through on lonely nights. Does she feel the same burning in her chest that I do? Does she believe in love at first sight? Shit, did I before our encounter?*

I reach for her hand and feel her pulse beating steady against my fingertips. She's cast a spell on me that I'm afraid will break, and I can't fathom this is the last time I'll share a moment like this with her—in bed, at peace, and happy for the first time in years.

Having loved before, I am wide awake at how different it feels with her. Launa is chill, easy, and light. No big entrances, no keeping up with the Joneses, no playing pretend that everything is perfect—even though she is quite close. I'll tell her this when she wakes. How, when I saw her, my heart skipped several beats as the sun cast a heavenly glow around her on the beach. How the sand swirled around her like magical dust, and her curly braids blew in the wind parallel to the wispy weeds behind her.

But first, my apology.

"Launa," I whisper, *feenin'* for more of her sugar the more I think about last night. "Launa," I call her name louder amidst a kiss I steal from the top of her head.

"Was I snoring?" she asks.

I roll her over to her back and kiss her navel. She giggles and jerks her stomach forward. I open my mouth and grip the hairs

2

above her passage in my teeth. She sighs and bucks her hips forward, feeding me her pussy. She's used to me already and wants me to revisit her wanton desires with the sucking, plucking, and tongue play I offered her last night.

Happily, I oblige to hear her moan, which sounds like melodic notes on a music staff. Together, she and I create a collage of songs from soul to rhythm and blues when our bodies collide, and our mouths expel the sighs and groans of electric euphoric ecstasy.

With ease, I spread her tan thighs and plant my face in her garden, watering her mowed lawn with a wet tongue lick, slow, sturdy, and sleek. She pushes my head down, and my tongue presses harder against her clit. "Oh," she whines with excitement when I circle it with my tongue, kiss it softly between my hungry lips, then flick it up and down like it's a switch I'm turning off, then on, off, then on.

Her heavy pants turn to low shrieks holding back a heightened cry out of shame. I wouldn't give a fuck if she woke the people in the room next to us—or the entire island—as long as it's my name she calls.

I slow down my taste for her with pitter-patter kisses up and down her saturated folds, squeezing her tiny ass cheeks like stress balls.

Finally, she mutters, "Levi. That feels good."

A moan overcomes a smile I try to hold back as I continue to gratify her. My lips nibble

3

on her left lip, then nibble on the right one. When she jolts, I gently snack on it, providing a warm kiss after each tug of her orifice, swallowing her juice dripping down my throat.

Her pussy responds well to my suction. My dick reacts to the sounds she makes. Her grunts, heavy pants, and moans cater to my ego that she enjoys the way I perform—approves of my delivery to her desirable needs.

I endure the pain of my hard dick tapping against my leg, impatiently waiting to part her pink sea. She's close to relieving her pearls.

I think.

I open and close two fingers like scissors below my wavering tongue inside her fountain. She's far from drenched and spazzing, yearning for more attention.

Rising to the occasion mentally and physically, my head slips into her world, and she gasps. Her back arches, lifting her supple breasts closer for me to suck. I stroke with intent, deep and swift, fucking her hard until we moan together and sing a new tune of sexual fulfillment to begin a new day.

My head slides between her breasts as she lowers her arched back to the bed. When I lift up, our eyes meet as the rhythm between us syncs to a memorable melody.

She's beautiful, staring up at me while I gaze into her baby browns. I poke, prod, and pierce her flesh, nearly losing it when she narrows her eyes and parts her lips, resting her teeth on the bottom one.

Then, she reaches for me, pulling me toward her. Her tongue draws mine into her mouth, and I apply pressure to her center. Her breath hitches between kisses, and chills prickle my back as her sighs motivate me to go deeper. Stroke harder. My senses tell me she prefers to fuck instead of make love, but I'm too afraid to ask her and ruin the memories we have yet to make.

I can't bear to lose what I've found, so I continue to perform as I have until she tells me otherwise.

"Fuck," I shout at Launa squeezing her walls so tight around me my dick feels stuck in a warm kaleidoscope.

I see colors and lose my edge as her moves ignite a rush in my bloodstream. The bag separating me from her true nature fills with my seeds, cutting my breath short as I cling to her body like a crazed shopper on Black Friday, scoring a hot item—which she is.

Feeling like the luckiest man in the world, I blurt out what's on my mind. "What are you doing for New Year's?"

Chapter 2

A Not-So-Cold Christmas

Launa

Seven Days Earlier

EIGHTY-DEGREE WEATHER AND FESTIVE string lights vined around palmetto trees is how we spend Christmas now. Babies hold power like infinity stones, dictating where the family celebrates the big holidays, and Lila, the one-year-old boss of the family, and the latest addition, TJ, call the shots like their mother has for as long as I can remember.

Long ago, I resented my big sister for that power, but my chest fills with justice from seeing the look on Landon's face when Daddy shoots past her to hold Lila in his arms.

"What are you grinning about?" Landon asks me.

"Sucks not being the favorite, doesn't it?"

She nudges my arm. "Whatever." Then, she skips past me to hug Mama.

I turn to Todd. "What time is sunset?"

"Not for a while. You missin' dreary skies already?"

I turn up my lip. "Home will always be home, but trekking in the sand versus mounds of snow has *got a* certain appeal."

"That it does. My toes get confused when I run in it without a pair of boots on my feet."

"I'm gonna go out there right now." I pick up Lila sitting next to my pops. "Timmy, come take a walk with us."

"Pass," he answers, his eyes glued to the television.

I kiss the baby boy's round face, then snuggle with my niece. "Let's go looking for dolphins, Sweet Cheeks."

The island is calm with beach music traveling from down the shore. There is a first time for everything, and it's my first time hearing Christmas tunes in the form of shag music. The feel-good rhythm stirs Lila to bounce in my arms.

"You like that, huh?"

She dances and wiggles herself down to my side. I hold her hand while she shuffles in the sand, and the gentle breeze of the ocean wraps around us.

Her squeaky voice yells, "You do it, Lala!"

I can't resist the order coming from the cutest face in the family. I swing our hands and shake my hips side to side, lost in her laugh and smile.

"Your daughter should be in commercials," a strong voice echoes above the incoming draft.

I turn toward the deep sound, hoping the face matches the tone. "Oh yeah," I say, peering at the brown man carrying sneakers in his hand.

A man in khakis? Never been down that road.

"I'd buy whatever she's selling if I had kids," he adds. "Or whatever product her mama is pushing."

I pause our dance session. "You always pour it on that thick, or am I special or something?"

"My apologies. I do tend to speak from the heart. I saw a beautiful woman with her beautiful child and couldn't help but pay a compliment. Sorry if I 'poured it on thick.' You two enjoy the rest of this beautiful day."

"You do the same."

I pick up Lila from playing in the sand and carry her toward the waves. My admirer looks back once he's left footprints in the mud for a few yards. He catches me staring at him and shows off his white teeth. I grin back, assuming he can't see my expression from that distance, then I turn away when the cold water sneaks to kiss my feet.

"Was he cute?" I ask my niece, burying her face against my shoulder from the winds picking up. The sky and clouds turn orange and red above us. "You truly are your mama's daughter," I say to her. "Can summon a man when you're not even trying." I laugh to myself. "You have no idea what I'm saying." I kiss her sugar-filled cheeks. "Let's head back. It's getting chilly all of a sudden."

Lila runs to her mother, who is swinging in a hammock on the porch. I stomp the sand out of my flip-flops on the top step.

Landon picks up the baby and holds her close. "The temperature changes quick out there, doesn't it?"

"It dropped, but it's nothing like what we're used to in the D."

"If I didn't know any better, I'd think you're starting to like it down here in slow Hilton Head."

"Would that be a bad thing?"

"Depends."

"On?"

She stands Lila up on her knees. "Adapting to change. Not being close to your loved ones."

"You talking about Mama and Daddy?"

She nods her head. "And you."

I plop down next to her on the hammock. It rocks back and forth as I hold onto the rope.

"I miss you, too. Especially this little version of cuteness you created." I tickle Lila's stomach. "We're gonna have to watch this one closely. She picks up men easy—like her mama."

"*Pssst.* Ha ha. I don't think Todd is ever going to let a boy get close to this one. And what are you talking about anyway?"

I peek through the gaps of the banister. "There was a man on the beach, shelling out compliments."

"What did he look like?"

"Taller than me, about six feet. Light brown. Had all of his hair from where I stood."

"Was he cute?"

"I think so. Maybe? I wasn't right up on him."

Landon chuckles. "Be careful of that. Remember the good and bad lighting episode of *Seinfeld*?"

Below my breath, I chortle. "That would be messed up if a color-changing sun made me imagine I met a nice-looking man walking barefoot on a beach."

Landon's judgmental brow rises. "Barefoot?"

"And wearing khakis."

"He doesn't sound like your type of hype." Her voice deepens and drags. "Or am I wrong? And just what did this random, shoeless, GAP-commercial man say to you?"

"Okay. Okay. I get it. We've entered joke territory. I'll see you inside."

I play a few games with Timmy and Todd before calling it a night. When the icky feel of dried sand rinses off my feet in the shower, a vision of the man from the beach flashes in my head.

His silhouette is faceless looking back at me. The vision is hazy, but I'm sure it's him. And in the manner of a dream, he manages to put a smile on my face.

Who was that guy?

Chapter 3

What's Mine Is Yours

Levi

I'M USED TO WAKING UP ALONE MOST mornings since the divorce, but I'll always hate how cold the other side of the bed feels—even on the nights I entertain company.

The women providing me with amusement this week are my two favorite aunts, bickering in the kitchen about how my grandfather likes his eggs.

"Mama used to add milk in them, and that's how Daddy likes them." Aunt Morgan bogarts the stove.

"But since we found out he's lactose intolerant, she stopped doing that." Aunt Lynnette snatches the milk from her hands.

"I know you didn't just—"

"Ladies." I interrupt them. "Good morning. Or can it be?"

"How you doin' Lee Baby?" Aunt Morgan perks up her lips to kiss my cheeks.

She's been doing this for as long as I can

remember. And never have my pleas for it to stop worked.

"You are just as much *my* baby." She squeezes my lips until they part, kisses one of my cheeks, then tells me, "Put some of that sugar in the Kool-Aid."

"I woke up this morning, so I'm doin' good. And Nana put extra cheese on his eggs when she stopped adding the milk," I add.

Aunt Lynnette scoffs and puts the milk back in the refrigerator. "I ain't never been able to tell that gal nothin'."

Aunt Morgan rolls her eyes. "Do you need us to go with you today?"

"Not this morning. But be camera ready this afternoon. A news reporter is stopping by to hear our side of the story."

"Your father would be proud to know you came home to help the family. He was something else in his day, but I declare you do take after him."

"That's sweet." I dip a fork into the scrambled eggs sizzling in the pan.

Aunt Morgan taps my arm with a towel. "Don't burn your mouth. Sit down and eat. No need to rush to the courthouse."

I blow the steam off the eggs, swallow them whole, and grab a juice. "No time to sit." I throw the fork in the sink and grab my keys off the nail near the door. "Don't forget about the interview."

"We won't," Aunt Lynette speaks for the both of them.

"Put your best wig on," I tease them on my way out the door.

The lawyers tell me not to worry about the lawsuit against my grandfather and our family home. I listen to him, but I can't help thinking about the lost battles against gentrification from nearby Charleston. The sickness has spread from the city, down to my grandparents' neck of the island. But I won't fold easily.

The cycle of stealing Black-owned acres of land and using underhanded tactics to sell lots right from under the original residents has never ceased. So much so that I can't say it's a historical act as it's still going on today.

My family was raised on the island. Once, a ninety-eight percent Black population post the Civil War thrived here. The former enslaved people owned and farmed the land now known as The Hamptons of the South. Most of it was lost due to the lack of proper inheritance wills, rising property taxes, and real estate greed forcing families off the land when they weren't left with clear title ownership, and became heirs' property owners.

Now the island has less than six percent of Black families that remain in the community, while the precious island has become a major attraction for tourists, developers, and land grabbers who disregard the Geechee Gullah heritage, and share one goal: gentrification.

I snap shots of the documents and hand them back to the attorney. "The papers are in order, so why is there a fight at all?"

"No question about it. The I's are dotted, and the T's are crossed. The deed belongs to your grandfather as sole owner since the passing of your grandmother. I asked to meet with you because he asked me to change the will."

"He did what?"

"He requested to leave all twenty acres of land to you. Good thing I hadn't filed the motion yet. We'd be stuck dealing with the transfer *and* this developer and his claims against the land."

"This is news to me. Maybe we should cancel the interview today."

"Oh no. We need that. National attention is great for this case. There's a long line of history being repeated here. Getting it out in the news will work in our favor."

I sigh. "We can hope."

"And I'll be present. Any questions you shouldn't answer...I'll intercept."

I reach forward to shake his hand. "Thanks for the information. I'll see you in a few hours."

I return to the house and sit with my grandfather shaping the bushes with an oval top around the windows.

"What they say, boy?"

"Not to worry. But you asked me to come down here and handle this mess, so I can't help but wonder what has you rattled with this case?"

He clips away at the shrubs. "Look 'round, son. I'm one of five people left 'round these

parts who own the very land his ancestors culti-
vated and raised their families on. If people
wasn't forced off, ran off, intimidated, or myste-
riously murdered, they sold it for a little of
nothing 'cause forty grand sounded good to 'em.
You and I know that's chump change, and this
land is worth millions. And I still wouldn't take
that. If them folk offer you five million, it's
worth twenty, if not more. I fear this devil
lurking 'round here is the first of many to try
and steal what's mine. And you can't trust
what's right will be ruled as such in these
courtrooms."

"Well, I looked over the papers today, and
everything should hold up in court."

"It should. But judges get paid off all the
time. Remember that pretty young gal, Chelle,
ya used to play wit' at *chuch*?"

I smile. "Yeah, I remember her. How is she
doing?"

"She'd be doing good if her brother didn't
agree with some family member who ain't
never seen these parts and was paid off to claim
ownership under that heirs' property mess and
sell *they* land under partition."

"What?"

"Yessa. Lost eight acres of land and had to
split forty thousand between the three of them.
She couldn't afford a lawyer, so your grandmother paid the fees for our attorney to represent her, and she was able to claim her
husband and two children in the split. That
didn't sit well with her brother and that

17

stranger, but it was all the justice she could get."

I shake my head. "I never liked her brother."

"Not many folk 'round here did."

"The lawyer told me your plans to put all of this in my name. Why not my aunties? They're your last living children."

"As if ya didn't hear them arguin' this mornin' over eggs. They would sell this place before I turned cold just not to be bothered wit' each other."

I fail to hide my laughter. "Daddy, you know those two are going to fight me if you do that."

"Why would I care? I'll soon be dead and resting in peace, knowing I didn't leave all this in the hands of someone who would sell it. And if *you* did sell it, I know you wouldn't be robbed by the man. I'd expect *you* to turn a major profit if you let it go."

"Daddy, don't say that. You could outlive me. You never know. And there isn't anywhere for me to work out here. My job requires being in places where there are actual things to investigate. *And* I don't have children. If something happens to me, then we could lose all of this under that heirs' law."

"You'll have children soon enough."

"And how do you know that?"

"Ya grandmother said she *seen* it before she died. And if ya don't, I know you'll still make sure this land is put to good use besides swinging a golf club on fake grass."

"I hear you, Daddy. I'm going back into town after the interview. Anything you want me to pick up for you while I'm over that way?"

"What you goin' back ova dey for?"

"I went for a walk on the beach yesterday to clear my head. It was relaxing."

Daddy gives me the side-eye. "Boy, I know times have changed according to what *I been* seein' on the TV, but if something ova dat way caught yo' eye...leave it ova dey. One of them kind would be just as happy to get *they* hooks into you comin' into this property."

"It's not like that. I did see a pretty girl out there yesterday, but she was probably married. And before you say anything, she was our kind of people."

"Humph. Must be a tourist, son."

"I didn't ask her, so I'll never know."

"Well, if lightnin' strikes twice, son, you betta take heed. She just might be the girl yo' grandmother saw in her dreams."

Chapter 4

Meddlesome

Launa

"You GIRLS WANT TO TAKE ME TO THAT farmer's market with the homegrown pickles?" Mama interrupts my joy of doing absolutely nothing.

"Now?" I ask.

"Yes, now. I've been wanting another jar of those things since the summer. And you know the freaks come out at night."

"I don't think that applies to this place, Ma."

"And I won't find out if it does or not. Let's go."

We stick out from the locals, but they treat us kindly because of all the praise my mother gives them. I hold her baskets as she fills them during her tour around the market, testing fruits, vegetables, treats, and small plates from every stand.

She won't admit it, but she enjoys coming down south—and not solely because of Landon and the babies. She likes the different climate

21

here on the coast. The continuous days of sunshine. Meeting new people. And this market with southern creations for her to explore.

"Let's grab a bite from that stand before we go back to the house." She points to a tent near a yellow house selling artwork out in front.

I stand behind her as she orders enough food to feed the house—Okra soup, fried corn on the cob, and a table-sized order of a seafood boil dinner to go.

"And we'll enjoy a brisket and barbecue at the table while we wait." Mama turns to me so I can pay.

I swipe my card and raise my brows at her. "Anything else, Mama?"

She sits at the table of her choosing. "I forgot to order that half lemonade, half sweet tea drink. I think that should cover it."

The woman behind the counter smiles as she passes me the receipt.

"Thank you," I say, then place the baskets on the bench. "Mama, how am I supposed to carry these baskets, *and* that grocery order you placed to the car by myself?"

"You can make two trips. I also want to buy one of those paintings to hang in Lila's room." She waves her hand towards the collection on the curb.

"So, in other words, Landon should have come with us to help me carry some of these things."

"Oh, hush that fuss." She clicks her tongue against the back of her teeth. "I have your sister

22

doing something else while you and I get to enjoy this beautiful day out."

"And what's that?"

"Babysitting your father." She chuckles.

I shake my head and snicker. "She is his favorite. They probably snuck out to do something together and left the kids with Todd."

"I hope they do. He misses her, ya know."

My face grimaces. "I know."

"You, too, since you've moved out. If you didn't let us keep Timmy on the weekends, I don't know if your father would've forgiven you. He's crazy about all of you kids—especially Timmy. He's the boy I never gave him."

"You talk as if I never come home."

"I know you do, but it's not the same as hearing your key hit the door during the hour of the devil." She rolls her eyes at me.

The cashier brings our order to the table. I slice each sandwich in half so Ma and I can share. She takes a total of three bites—one of the brisket and two of the barbecue—then wraps them up.

"I sampled so much today I can barely eat all of this."

"And you've ordered so much food to go we won't have to cook until Christmas Day."

"Good. We did come down here to relax." She exhales a deep breath. "Put my food in the bag when the girl brings out the to-go order."

"I better make the first trip to the car. Be right back."

I load the trunk with the baskets of goodies

and return to my mother making friends with some man in a tank top, jean shorts, and dark-red tanned legs.

"Launa, this nice gentleman was just telling me they have a concert tonight at one of the resorts on the beach."

"Is that right?"

"And it's free to the public." He hands me his business card. "My band would love it if you all could make it and celebrate the holidays with us."

I grin at my mother. "You realize it won't be church Christmas music, right?"

She fans me off. "We'll be there."

"Pardon me for intruding." I hold up my hands. "I'll go grab the painting you want while you two chat."

"Grab the second one from the left with the blue butterfly."

I sass her with a raised tone of voice. "Nothing for the baby?"

Her eyes remain focused on the man while she answers me. "His day is coming." She shoos me away.

♡

Mama's new friend is gone when I return to the table with the painting. She skims over the drawing as if she was an expert at a gallery in another life.

"Lila Bean is going to love this," she says.

The cashier from the food truck unloads our massive order in the center of the table.

Mama chuckles below her breath. "Well, it looks like you'll be making three trips to the car."

I sigh. "Sit tight, boss lady. I'll come back for you and your butterfly."

"Lightning has struck twice." A deep voice pulses my chest.

My mother peeks over the painting.

A mild scowl appears above my brows. "Excuse me?"

"Launa, who is this man?" Mama asks.

"I don't know," I lie, studying him up close. "Who are you?"

He extends his hand. "Levi King. I saw you, and I assume, your daughter on the beach yesterday."

Mama butts in. "She doesn't have a daughter."

"That was my niece."

"Forgive me. She was just as pretty as you, so I thought..."

Mama interjects, "Launa has a son."

"Launa." He smiles.

I give Mama a sharp eye.

"Well, either way, she's a beautiful baby." His eyes meet with mine. "Looks seem to run in the family."

"My, my, my. Aren't you a smooth one." Ma snickers. "You don't sound like you're from this island."

"My roots are here, but I grew up in North Carolina."

I hold his gaze. "So you're home for the holidays?"

"I'm actually in town on business."

"What kind of business?"

"Stopping a steal, in layman's terms."

"Oh?" My mother frowns.

"A big corporation is trying to bully my grandfather out of the family land. I'm here helping him fight off the wolves until they go back to where they came from."

"So, you're some kind of lawyer, then?"

"No, ma'am. I work in real estate. Mainly property preservation, but I also offer private investigation services for a firm based out of Charleston where I currently reside."

"Sounds complicated," I say, observing him closely to see if he fidgets or has a tell for when he lies.

He pulls out his card. "This is for you."

"Why? I'm not looking at properties down here."

"You might one day."

"I'm a city girl. It's too slow down here for me."

"And what city is that?"

"Detroit."

Mama chimes in. "Born and raised in Flint. She's closer to the city now."

"I've never been to Michigan."

"Whatchu afraid of?"

"Nothing. I never had any business there."

I tap his card.

"Until now." Levi's face goes blank with guilt that he said the quiet part out loud.

"Ha!" Mama cackles.

Levi's embarrassment grows from her laugh and he stammers, "I mean..."

"Ma!" I grit through my teeth, praying her chuckles settle.

"If you're firm about not ever leaving the city, I hope you still use the number on there." He points to his card. "I'd love it if you used it before you head back to Detroit. I was thinking I could take you to dinner, or maybe show you around while you're in town."

Mama clears her throat. "Back in my day, the man did the calling."

Levi smiles at her. "Times have changed ma'am. Women are supposed to do full background checks on men before giving out their information. If your daughter gives me the green light, I'll call her nonstop."

Mama raises her brows. "Tuh. I see." A curve lifts from the corner of her mouth as she turns to me. "Baby girl, I reckon you better get to checkin' before this one is taken off the market."

I eye him up and down. "Are you...off the market? A girl has to ask these days."

"I'm as single as a dollar bill."

Chapter 5

Dinner for Two

Levi

SHE'S A CUTIE PIE. PETITE WITH A SASSY walk, and lips the color of salmon with a light shine to them. If I were cocky, I'd kiss them on sight to taste the flavor of her lip gloss mildly shining from the stage lights of a show she's invited me to. It's not the dinner I had in mind, but it's comforting to know she's not pretentious and high maintenance right off.

Been there, done that.

There's something about her that makes me feel alive again. Like I want to tell her my deepest, darkest secrets and aim to give her the world. I feel nervous standing close to her, crafting my words carefully as if I'll say the worst thing ever and lose my chance to get to know her.

So far, I can tell she's cool. Like the popular girl in high school who other girls secretly want to be like. The down-to-earth girl everyone gets along with. The girl that everyone laughs at her jokes and watches when she walks in a room.

I'm lucky she called, because she's definitely cooler than me.

"Do you like this kind of music?" she asks.

Lie.

"Um. It's cool."

Enough with the cool, man. Just lie and say you like it.

"I've never heard Christmas music like this in a live show. It's not too shabby," she adds.

"I have no complaints. I'm just happy to be here—with you."

"Should we grab a table?"

"If we can find one."

My eyes set on an abandoned table below a luau ring of flowers with mistletoe stuck in it. I pull out a chair for her, then sit opposite her for a perfect view.

She catches me off guard and says, "Your background checked out quite nicely. Mind if I ask about your divorce?"

"Not at all. I ignored the red flags and was taken for a ride. My ex-wife was quite the character—still is, from what I hear."

Launa tightly presses her lips together before adding, "Still is, huh? You keepin' tabs on your ex?"

"Nah, nothing like that. We share a circle of friends who like to tell the latest gossip is all. Let's just say karma is dealing with her pretty good right now."

Launa scoffed. "She hurt you, didn't she?"

"She did. But she also taught me a few lessons."

"Such as?"

"What kind of woman not to get involved with going forward, and how to communicate so I don't make the same mistakes twice. How about you? Any lessons an ex taught you?"

Her fingers fidget on the table. "Oh yeah."

"I'm all ears."

"The most important lesson was to know my worth. The hardest lesson was patience."

"You seem quite worthy to me. Hope I'm right about that hunch."

Her cheeks flush.

I signal for the waitress, then ask Launa, "How long are you in town?"

"We fly out on the 27th."

"You guys go hard for Christmas?"

"You can say that. We don't do caroling or anything, but we open gifts as a family, cook big dinners, bake lots of treats, watch all the movies, and drink like there is no tomorrow."

"Sounds like a good time. I haven't spent Christmas here in years. My family rotates where we spend it each year, and the occasion isn't always peaceful. My aunts bicker, my cousins scheme, and I spend most of my time hiding from everyone until my grandmother would summon all of us to dinner. May she rest in peace. Then, I'd hide again."

She laughs. "So your family is spicy. Ain't nothing wrong with that."

I find myself opening up to her as if she was an old friend. I tell her more about my failed marriage, my friends I want her to meet, and the anxiety I feel about resolving my family's property claim.

She offers a lending ear and often engages to let me know she's listening. I am beaming inside that I haven't bored her or lost her interest, especially since she won't share much about herself when I ask.

We finish our meal of appetizers and mixed libations, then head out toward the water. The heavy breeze blows me into her as she tugs on her sweater near her neck.

I make a bold move and wrap my arm around her shoulder. "I didn't expect it to be this chilly out here. We can go back inside if you want."

"This is nothing compared to where I'm from. The breeze is a little different, but not the temperatures. I can tolerate it for a little while."

She snuggles into me, and we look up at the open sky at the same time.

"Are you an astrology guy, by chance?"

"I know nothing about the stars except the big and little dipper. Occasionally, I may take interest in an article telling you what's in the sky tonight. Other than that, I'm clueless."

She points into the void. "See how those stars curve?"

I lie and say, "Yes."

"Now look slightly to the left and below that curve. Can you make out a trapezoid in the stars?"

I squint my eyes, searching for the constellation.

Her finger circles the air as if it's a map she can touch. "The curve is right there, then below it to the left is a trapezoid shape."

I widen my eyes back to normal, and suddenly the outline appears. "Holy shit. I actually see it. What is it?"

"That's Leo. That's me. And don't ask me to show you another sign because I only know mine." She laughs.

"Well, from one Leo to another, thank you. I have never seen my zodiac in the stars before."

"When is your birthday?"

"The fourteenth."

"I'm on the first."

We share a moment I don't want to end.

"Launa, I'm going to sound weird right now, but I hope this date isn't over anytime soon."

"I'm having a good time myself, but there isn't much to do around here this time of night, unless we go back inside and close the house down with the cover band—but then what?"

Chapter 6

Never-ending

Launa

WE PHYSICALLY FLIRT ON THE DANCE FLOOR as the songs change from upbeat Christmas classics accompanied by added jingles to the tunes.

The lead singer steps aside as one of the back-up singers replaces him centerstage. Her bushy blonde curls stand taller than the microphone, but her presence commands attention from every local in house.

The band slows down the tempo of the room. Levi and I look at each other in shock. He doesn't ask, but I waltz into his arms as he holds me close, humming along to the band's rendition of "*What Do the Lonely Do at Christmas?*"

"She sounds good, doesn't she?" he says between riffs.

"Damn near identical to *The Emotions*."

"I've been playing this song for the past few years during the holidays. I hope that phase comes to an end."

"That would be nice," I say, and lay my head against his sweater.

I listen to the rest of the song with one ear and to his heartbeat with the other. His grip around my back sends chills down my spine and creates stirrings of a sexual nature in my body.

I snap out of my mischievous mind and look at him. The song has ended, but his hold on me remains the same.

"Sorry." I apologize. "I didn't realize the slow dance was over."

"For about a few minutes now, but I wouldn't dare interrupt how good you feel this close to me."

I clear my throat. "Shall we stand here and continue to be the spectacle or..."

He takes my hand and leads us back to our table. He leaves a tip below the plate of picked over potato skins and escorts me to his car.

When he opens my door, he pauses, tickling my fingertips with slow brushes. I close my eyes and wait to feel his lips against mine. His warm hand strokes my cheek before pushing back my hair that is blowing in my face from the harsh wind.

The notes of a citrusy cologne drape closer and closer above me as I take a breath seconds before his lips plant onto mine. They taste like a sweet mango infused with vodka and grenadine. We swap kisses in a fiery exchange, neither pulling away. I no longer remember it's chilly outside. I'm warm and turning hotter by the second, on the verge of being the fast-ass girl I promised I would no longer be.

Murmurs from a couple walking in the lot distract me from the sweetness of his kiss. The woman laughs as the car door alarm beeps to let her in. Finally, I retreat from him and look toward the car door closing.

He rubs his clean-shaven face against mine. "Where do you want to take this?"

"I'm in your stomping grounds. You tell me."

"Feel like taking a drive?"

"I'd love to."

He drives me around the neighboring towns, explaining it's the scenic route to Savannah, Georgia. It looks like we're passing the same trees for miles until we hit the small city. *I've never seen so many churches in my life*, I say to myself as Levi tells me how good the food is here, then throws in a curveball about ghost tours we should go on.

"No, thanks. I don't play with the dead. But I'll happily go on a food tour if that's an option."

"Am I hearing you've agreed to let me take you on a second date?"

I smile as I scoff. "Yes."

"Day after Christmas sound good?"

"Yeah."

"Then, I can show you the famous oak trees everyone comes here to see."

"I've seen the ones with the white moss draping across them in the movies. That would be a cool pic to show my lil' man before my sendoff."

"I hope it won't be the last time I see you," he says.

While we cruise around the dead city and a gazillion cemeteries and parks, I take every moment of silence between us to think about the good time I'm having with him. How I'm enjoying being in his company, listening to him talk about things I have zero interest in, like oak trees, slave trivia embedded in him having been raised on the soil where it was prevalent, and how the butterflies in my stomach have been swirling since we kissed.

It's 4 a.m. when he parks outside Landon's house. He keeps the engine running on half a tank of gas to keep me warm while he shares old stories of his summers as a child on the island, and what it was like when he moved here permanently as a teen to finish high school, and makes me laugh at his witty jokes. He's actually pretty funny.

His eyes light up when he looks into mine. It only takes a second for our lips to touch for the second time.

Heat grows between us, and I want him to take me, but I fight off my urges to straddle him in the car on our first date.

Behind the condensation fogged on the windows, I notice a light is now on in the living room in the house.

I point to it. "Someone's up now."

He giggles. "Well, the sun *is* coming up."

He points to the blurry orange line resting between an ever-changing blue sky and green water on the beach.

"Janet was right. Time does fly when you're having fun." I lean over and kiss him one more time. "Call me later?"

"I plan on it."

2

Mama rolls her eyes at me when I enter the kitchen to snag a biscuit.

"What?" I ask with a smile on my face.

"Don't 'what' me. I just hope you kept both feet on the floor."

"Ma!" I say, nearly choking on the dough. "And yes," I answer her with a mouth full.

"Good."

"For now," I mumble.

"What was that?"

"I said goodnight. Save me one of these for later, please. I'm going to take a nap."

I wake to Todd grinning at me and Landon judging me as usual.

"Where are the kids?"

Landon narrows her eyes at me. "Outside with Daddy."

"You got a glow about you this mornin', lil' sis." Todd chuckles.

"Don't play with me. Nothing happened."

"You sure about that? We haven't seen you since yesterday," Landon jokes.

"Ha ha. Nothing happened."

T.K. RICHARDS

"I take it you had a nice time, then."

The biggest smile graces my face. "I had a lovely time *without* giving up the goods—yet."

"So khaki man has game?"

"You can say that." I turn up my lip. "He's not the kind I used to go for. I've learned my lesson, I guess."

"You gonna let us meet him?"

"Mama met him."

"So." Landon looks at Todd. "Invite him over for dinner tomorrow night."

"On Christmas? I'm sure he has plans with his own family."

"Then how about tonight?" Landon suggests. "The four of us could go out for drinks and leave the kids here with Mama and Daddy."

I turn to Todd for help.

"Don't look at me. Your sister has been in my ear about this all morning."

I sigh. "I'll ask him."

Chapter 7

Meet The Family

Levi

AT MY REQUEST, LAUNA MAKES A QUICK appearance to meet my family rolling in for Christmas. I introduce her to my cousins hanging outside, then whisk her away when they spark up a joint.

She whispers, "Why'd you do that?"

"It's a trap for them to talk about you later with my mother."

"Okay. Thanks for the save. But I should tell you I don't mind partaking. Is that a problem? Being that you are almost a cop and stuff."

"It's not. I don't think there's much you can do to turn me off."

We enter the house, and my family turns to us in the same fashion as the folks watching us linger on the dance floor the previous night.

"Bring her in here." My aunt waves us inside.

My mother stands at the table. "Launa, meet my mother, Mrs. King."

Launa bypasses a handshake and goes in for a hug. "Nice to meet you."

My mother's eyes grow big as she stares at me over her shoulder. "Levi said you were pretty. He was right. Nice of you to join us."

I cut in. "We're not joining you, Ma. I told you her family is getting together tonight. She was kind enough to swing by to meet everyone while they are here."

"Oh, I see. That is rather sweet and generous of you."

"Levi has been so kind to me. I had to meet the woman who raised such a gentleman."

"He is my pride and joy."

Granddaddy taps Launa on the shoulder. "You must be the one my wife saw coming."

"Granddad," I stress through gritted teeth.

"I'm sorry." Launa stares between the two of us. "Levi, what is he talking about?"

"I'll explain later." I sigh. "This is my grandfather, Logan King. Daddy meet Launa."

"So good of you to join us."

"Thank you for having me."

My impatient Aunt Morgan eases over. "What's this about you can't stay?"

"Uh, my folks have a little something planned."

"You should have brought them with you," my mother adds.

"Ma." I frown.

"Well, maybe next year. How about it?"

Launa nods. "That sounds like a plan. Even though I can't stay and my mother has cooked enough to feed a starting line-up, would I offend you if I ask to take a plate with me to go?"

"Sure!" every woman in the house answers at once.

"And two pieces of cake, please. Levi bragged about a red velvet cake one of you makes that should win awards, and I told my mother about it. She will kill me if I come back without a slice for her."

"Does your mother bake?" Aunt Lynette asks.

"Yes. Recipes from an old cookbook her grandmother handed down to her. Her specialty is a caramel cake that melts in your mouth."

"Levi, you bring me a slice of that cake, ya hear?" Aunt Lynette demands.

As my family packs Launa two plates of food and dessert, I introduce her to everyone in the house, then walk her back to her car.

"Thanks for showing face tonight." I open her door.

Launa takes the foil-covered plates and Styrofoam dinners from my hand. "I wish I could stay, but..."

"I wish I could leave with you..." I ease closer and pin her against the car.

"See you for dinner tomorrow night?"

"I'm counting the minutes already."

I press my lips against hers and hold them there until her mouth opens. Our tongues coil, and we share the air surrounding us as we barely come up for it, panting from high emotion.

Whistles travel from the yard. We pull away and laugh.

"See you tomorrow." I smooch her one more time. "I gotta go punch my stupid cousin."

"How do you know which one was teasing you?"

"Every family has that one person who stirs up shit."

She laughs. "That's true. Me and that cousin have a lot in common." She climbs inside and takes off.

♡

My family fills every room at my grandparents' home, while Launa's family has plenty of space to roam in her sister's house, being a small unit of eight. It leads me to wonder if she wants more children. *Has she drawn the line at her son? Would she give me a child of my own?*

Her mother compliments the red velvet cake. "Tell your aunt she makes a mean cake. If I could take one with me on my flight, I would."

"She'll hold that over my mother's head until next Christmas."

"We'll be gone the day after tomorrow, but be sure and send word by Launa if she likes that caramel cake I'm sending back with ya."

"Yes, ma'am."

The newborn cries, and Launa jumps up to tend to him. Her sister exhales her thanks as

Mr. Davis finally acknowledges me since we exchanged hellos.

"So, young man, I heard what you're doing for your folks. I wish you luck with that. The government is nine times out of ten in cahoots with these corporations. They can be downright dirty."

"They have been to many around here. I can't allow my family to fall victim, though."

"Determination. That's good for a man to have," he adds.

"Tell me, Levi." Todd joins in as his daughter bounces on his knee. "What do you investigate?"

"Mostly fraud. Spousal disputes when dividing assets, and mortgage fraud between lenders and homeowners. Most recently I helped uncover discrimination where a brokerage firm undervalued a home because the owners were Black. Before that, I helped a couple win a suit for racial separation, where a firm had its agents refuse to take clients who look like us on house tours, and when they did, it was never in the locations that were requested. On top of that, they subjected the Black clients to ridiculously high financial qualifications, but not their white clients."

"Only our kind, huh?"

"Well, when we broke down the results on a pie chart, 50% of Black clients were victims, 30% Latin clients fell prey, and 20% Asian clients were hit."

Landon sucks her teeth. "Why am I not surprised by those numbers."

"What's your experience been like 'round here?"

"You mean since most of the residents don't look like us?" Todd glances at his wife. "We haven't had any issues. The neighbors seem nice enough, but my wife and I are actually thinking about moving to Charleston. We went to a festival and caught a few shows down there and liked it. There's a lotta money to be made down there."

Mrs. Davis stands with her hands on her hips. "When were you going to tell us?"

"When we settle on a property." Todd narrows his eyes at Landon.

"We found one that suits us perfect," she confesses.

"But?" Launa asks.

"It has a guest house in the back, and we were going to propose that Mama and Daddy move down here."

"And leave me back home by myself?" Launa gives Landon the evil eye.

A brief silence fills the dining room.

"No, not leave you back home. There's enough land to build another house on the lot. We could have our own little compound," Landon explains. "I'm thinking of generational wealth. Solid property. Private land. We pass down the homes to our children and so forth."

Todd raises a finger. "I saw a documentary about living in the east, and parents are now building homes with preparation that their children will have to live with them. It's hard out here. Why not be prepared in case times get even harder. Plus, we'll all have our own house, but still be together."

"And what about your business?" Mr. Davis inquires.

"I'll keep it outside Savannah as long as it's making money. If we move, I'm going to open a warehouse and a second location. Landon's pillow orders have been picking up, and we have some other avenues we're thinking about exploring. Having our own warehouse could be real lucrative."

I reach across the table to shake Todd's hand. "I like how you and the Mrs. move. We should get together and talk business sometime." I smile at Launa.

Her lips press together to hide a wistful smile. "Let's go outside."

She hands the baby to Mr. Davis, then takes my hand. As we walk toward the door, I overhear Mrs. Davis chastise Landon.

"I wouldn't mind, but you and your sister on the same property...I don't know. She may have to buy a house close by, like down the street or something. You know you two don't always get along."

"We have lately," says Landon. "She just reacted that way because she thought we were leaving her out."

Launa looks back and shuts the door behind us. My eyes set on her and she brings a huge smile to my face.

"What is that smile for?" she asks.

"It seems my card just might come in handy after all."

She pokes my chest and sinks her teeth into her bottom lip. "Shut up and kiss me."

I don't hesitate. I pull her in close by the small of her back and taste the leftover strawberry flavor on her lips. They're sticky and soft but delightful all the same, stirring up an erection pressing against her.

She jerks back. "Well, hello."

"Whatever you do, don't take me back inside until I'm presentable."

She giggles. "Yeah, I wouldn't do you like that. Both of my parents seem to like you."

"Your whole family's cool."

"Surprisingly. The baby-making machine likes you, too. She's never this warm with anyone I bring around this fast. You're quite the charmer." Launa pulls on my zipper.

"And you're quite the snake charmer." I'm drawn to the sexy manner in which she bites her lip. "Fuck it. You wanna grab a room at that hotel we went to last night?"

She releases my belt. "You go tell my parents goodbye while I kiss my son goodnight."

Chapter 8

Loose Khakis

Launa

His hand rests on my thigh for the short drive to the hotel. With it being the holiday season, tourism is slow and guarantees us a room. He leaves me in the lot to check-in, then returns to the car.

"Suite on the top floor," he says, holding up the key card.

"Nice."

'I'm glad he knows I'm worth the splurge for one night of erotic pleasure.'

Somewhere between dinner and the lock securing the door, the nice guy I swapped kisses with transforms into an aggressive wild animal.

"Forgive me for tonight," he says, pressing his hands against my ass, coaxing me to the bed.

An intense gaze into my eyes prepares me for his early request of absolution. It tells the story of what will transpire overnight. I grow excited. Eager. Energized. Starved.

I brace myself for long bouts of foreplay—I

expect it, honestly. His good manners make him a good candidate for being an undercover freak, and I grow weary in proving myself right.

He kisses me hard as his hands mesh with the cold skin of my back. My bra becomes un-attached before I'm led to lie back on the bed. I feel a trickle of warmth saturate the lining of my panties when his bulge rocks against me. Suddenly, I remember how good being hunched feels. The anticipation of being plucked like a flower. Erupting urges stacking like a cemented wall ready to be knocked down.

The more he grinds on me in the midst of owning my tongue and sucking the mint lip balm off my lips, the more I throw my hips forward, enjoying the friction building between us.

The torment of not indulging into battle on the mattress right away makes me spiral. A sudden jolt of his fingers pinching my nipple below my top escalates my need to be explored.

His mouth escapes mine and dives south. His teeth bite my nipple gently, pricking a tiny hole in my sweater, until he exposes them from the bondage of layers.

He sucks, and he sucks, then groans. "They're perfect," he says, tracing the deeper brown of my skin with his tongue.

As he sucks on one nipple, he tweaks the other to my delight. Becoming overheated, I slide off my sweater with the bra attached at the arms.

"I was getting to that, but your skin tastes so good I couldn't help myself." He slides my pants past my ankles. "Let's see if you're sweet everywhere," he adds, holding eye contact between us until I fold, losing myself at the fondling of his tongue softly wavering on my orifice.

He snacks on me as if he practiced a routine of what he would do to me when given the chance.

"Don't stop," I beg.

He hums, "I won't," lathering my entrance until I shriek between bouts of holding my breath.

He pulls back. "I like hearing you make that sound."

I wait to feel the warmth of his tongue continue to play with my pussy. Instead, I feel a finger trace my slit as he kisses my inner thigh.

Slowly, his lips travel back to where he is missed. He examines me up close, massaging the secret line between the hood of my folds. The slickness creates a slippery sensation for his fingers to massage the lines with ease. I moan at the sensual kneading sending me to euphoric heights.

"I think you like that," he whispers.

"How can you tell?" I grin.

"The look on your face. The sound your pussy is making."

I blush of embarrassment and sigh from being fulfilled. He moans at the gushy sound of music he's making using my body as his instrument. I then lose restraint of silencing my cries when his wet fingers divest from my barrier, and his thumbs softly rotate against my clit like it's a punching bag.

"Unh," I cry out and curl up, holding his gaze as he watches me fall into abandon.

It's hard to look away as his stare holds me captive. Melting me mentally. Connecting our minds like waves invisible to the eye seeping between him and me.

"Anytime you want me to do this, all you've got to do is ask, baby. You hear me?" His sincere voice leads me to believe him.

I can't speak I'm so far gone. Turned on from the look of mischief in his eyes. The touch of his caress. My hunger for him choking my voice.

"You hear me?"

I finally nod as faint squeals escape my throat.

He turns me to my side and raises my leg, kissing my calf until he reaches my inner thigh. His tongue glides sideways between my ass and my pussy, compelling me to ball my fist as I hold my chest.

His nose graces my asshole while his chin nearly presses in my hole.

"My God," I murmur into my fist, holding myself as I lose strength from his wide chin mildly fucking me and teasing me into submission. The farther it pushes inside, my shoulders shiver.

"Ah," I expel.

"Umph, umph, umph." His voice vibrates in my tunnel. "Thatta girl," he says, watching me milk. He tastes what I've produced. "The verdict is in. You are sweet everywhere," I hear him say over the tearing sound of a wrapper.

The khakis drop above his shoes, and I hold back my giggle. He kicks off everything trapped below his knees, then s*mack*, the condom cuffs the base of his shaft. I exhale, desperately in need of a breather, unprepared he would plunge inside without a warning. Without ease.

I receive, and he gives willingly, withdrawing gasps of pain and pleasure from my lips. My body hasn't felt this wonderful in months. Or ever. I grow dizzy, trying to compare the experience with the lovers of my past.

He digs and drills mercilessly, swirling his dick in every corner he can research. My pussy clamps and gyrates of rewarded ecstasy from the diligence of his service taking over my body.

My thighs are nudged by his palm. He spreads my legs wide into a split while holding them prisoner at the knees. I exhale a deep breath.

"I need you to take it like this." He pokes deep. "Show me you can handle me."

I close my eyes to take the beating.

"That's it, my sweet angel. Take all of me."

I quiver.

"Ah, yes, Launa. Give it all to me," he whispers. "A good girl with some good pussy." His voice breaks as he winds freely inside of me.

I endure the aching strokes, pushing back on his chest. To avoid ruin, I summon him to kiss me. He lowers down and obeys.

I maneuver him to his back and ride him like the bull he is without falling off. His eyes beam, watching me work him over as his fingers trace the brown skin surrounding my nipples. When he pinches them, my pussy clenches.

"I fucking love that shit," he moans, then pinches them again. "I could never tire of you." He places a finger in my mouth and moves his other hand to my hip.

Throwing me an assist, *and* to fuck me harder, he uses his hand placed on my hip to sway my pussy around his dick. I like that move, creating an intense pressure, securing my ass in place so I can't slip off him.

"I...I..." I croon.

"Yes, you are," he says, circling my clitoris with the finger that exits my mouth.

I'm glued to him, unloading like ice cream on his cone while he is still in play.

His hand leaves my hip and wraps around my throat as he strokes vigorously from below to join me in pure pleasure.

He roars, "Goddamn, Launa!"

I get off to the sound of a gratified man calling my name. It makes me feel like I own him. Like he's been tamed. Like he's mine.

Hours later, it is morning, and we're at it again.

"Housekeeping," the cleaning staff shouts over a knock.

We ignore her and carry on with a repeat of lustful, shaming acts neither of us can deny. I'm floating, having been tuned up for the first time in a long while. The happiness exuding from his energy tells me he is all the same.

From the bed to the little chair oddly placed near the middle of the room, I give myself to him. Bent over with his nose stuffed up my ass, I close my eyes as his tongue strides long and deep, covering every inch of my hidden places.

I squeeze the pillows decorating the chair to gag my moans from the penetration of his comely dick treading my waters. I'm in heaven, enraptured, beguiled by his dedication to please me.

We come together and order room service, enjoying breakfast overlooking the rushing waves while draped in plush, white robes.

Levi grins with a mouth full of food. I raise a brow to hear what he's holding back, and he points his fork at me.

"What are my chances of holding you captive until your flight tomorrow?" He stares as my eyes roam. "What does that look mean?"

"I'm thinking of what all I have to pack, and I'm picturing the look on my mother's face when I take my walk of shame."

"Are you...ashamed?"

I shake my head. "Not in the least."

"Neither am I." He sighs aloud.

"Since we've skipped all the bases and went straight for the homerun." I tighten the belt of my robe and chuckle. "And we're here in these plush rented robes, I was wondering—what did you have planned for the date we're already on?"

Levi chortles. "We can still go out, if you want to. I wanted to keep my word and show you those landmarks, but then I looked into taking you on a hibachi boat cruise where we could witness the sunset while floating on the open water. Unfortunately, it was sold out."

"Can we do that the next time I visit?"

"I'll plan ahead." He smiles at me. "So what about tonight? Wanna go for that drive and take that picture in front of the famous oak tree?"

"Next time. Tonight, I'm good with getting your money's worth in this room."

We stay in each other's company and take a stroll on the beach, explore intimacy in the shower, and run up the hotel bill with food, champagne, and movies.

Cuddled in each other's arms, we fall asleep before midnight, awakened when the sun creeps between the curtains just in time for us to enter a final round of laborious fucking as a lasting memory.

Levi rolls from on top of me, heavily breathing and grunting. "What are you doing for New Year's?"

I lift up. "What'd ya have in mind?"

"I wanna spend it with you."

Chapter 9

New Year's

Levi

LAUNA FALLS ASLEEP ON MY SHOULDER ON the plane. My arm needs to move, but I resist the urge not to wake her peaceful state.

When she wakes, I stretch and ask her, "Is there anything in particular you want to do while we're here? Take a tourist pic in one of those red phone booths, eat fish and chips, or visit one of those high tea houses?"

"There is a Black-owned tea house I was told to try. We can go there. Other than that, I'm following your lead, since you've been here before."

"Buckingham Palace isn't open this time of year, but we can drive past it."

She rolls her eyes at me. "My girl is in California. I'll pass."

I snicker. "Your girl."

She raises a brow at me. "You heard me."

"Yes, ma'am. I did."

We exit the plane and meet the driver of a car Max and Nadia has waiting for us at curbside. Launa's thigh pulls my hand to it like a magnetic attraction once I'm belted in the back seat.

"I missed you. Have I told you that already?"

She places her hand to her neck. "You didn't say it in words, but I got the message. The flowers, the late Christmas present—these tickets."

"I gather you like the necklace."

Her fingers circle the pendant. "I liked the note, too."

I beam from the inside. "Thank you for accepting my invitation."

"Maybe I missed you, too."

She allows me to kiss her with the chauffeur watching us from the rearview mirror. As excitement begins to build from the softness of her strawberry lips rushing blood to the front of my pants, I pull back.

Launa wipes the residue of her lipstick from my lips. "So, what hotel are we staying at?" she asks as he begins to drive us out of the city limits.

"We're staying at a house."

"Like an Airbnb?"

"Nope, you'll see."

Her eyes are wide, taking in the foreign land while the sun sets. I sense she's nervous now that the city lights have turned into open road and rural terrain.

An hour later, we arrive at the Sharpers'

mansion. She takes a huge gulp, bites her lip, and turns to me.

I say nothing, and stare at her brown eyes as they narrow at me.

"What is this place?"

I rub my hands together. "My best friends live here."

"And what, they just let you roll up whenever you choose?"

"Pretty much. When I come into town, they let me stay in the guest house." I point to the lowly lit lights nearly invisible behind a row of trees.

She scoffs and adjusts her legs. "What do these friends do exactly?"

"Nadia is a writer, and Maximus is in music. He deejays, does movie scores, and produces a slew of famous artists known around Europe. Some international."

"*Well*, I didn't think I could feel under-accomplished around anyone more than I do my sister." She blinks as her head jolts with an astounded expression on her face. "I stand corrected."

I scowl. "Is that how you see yourself? Under-accomplished?"

"Every day since I've been walking in Landon's shadow. She's the successful one. She left a big job, moved down south, and started making pillows, for Christ's sake. And she's excelling at it." She chuckles. "I left a shitty nine-to-five to substitute teach at my son's school to be close by with all the madness going on."

"Which is admirable. And something a good mother would do, which makes *you* successful."

She narrows her eyes at me. "You're being sweet. Thanks."

"I'm being honest. *And* a little sweet."

She finally smiles showing all her teeth when the car stops. Maximus walks down the steps and lets his two-year-old son run amuck as the driver helps me unload our bags from the trunk.

Nadia opens the front door. "Tre! Come back inside!" she calls to her boy. "Levi, you're here! I'll see you inside!"

"Brother." Maximus pounds my back. "It's good to have you back."

"How you been, man?"

"Brilliant." He reads my eyes, then turns to Launa. "You must be Launa. Levi has told us all about you."

She blushes. "Has he?"

"Yeah. The wife and I hope you feel at home here. Any friend of Levi's is a friend of ours. You two must be tired. Let's get you settled inside, yeah?"

I take her hand and we follow Maximus. Nadia greets us at the door and points to glasses filled with wine on the table beside her.

"I've prepared for this visit, chased behind two busy-bodies, and haven't slept in days. I deserve this glass and thought you two should join me after a long trip." She glances over Launa. "Especially you, since your journey was the longest. If you don't drink red, I have plenty of other options. Come on in."

Launa lifts her glass and raises it to Nadia. "I like your style already."

They lead us to the family room on the first floor. Launa's face expresses nothing short of amazement as we pass through the wide halls and rich decorum on the walls.

Nadia hugs me. "Levi, we know you normally have the house out back to yourself, but Mother Sharper and her sister will be here tomorrow to watch the kids. They can handle the little ones better in that house, so we were hoping you'd agree to stay in here with us. You two will have this floor to yourselves and still have privacy. We'll only share the kitchen."

"When have you ever known me to complain?"

"Never."

Mash pats my back and says to Launa, "He's such a good egg."

Launa hold her lips tight with champagne in her mouth and raises her brows. "Hm," she moans.

Nadia adds, "If she doesn't know that yet, she will soon enough." She winks at Launa, then leans into Mash. "It'll be good to have you two in the house with us anyway. We miss you. Especially, Tre." She looks down at her son pulling at my leg.

I pick him up. "Where's Cassia?"

Nadia points to the pillows on the sofa. "Hiding," she whispers. "Now, you and Mash take these kids and tire them out so they can go to bed, while me and Launa here get turned up."

"Who is Mash?" Launa asks.

"My husband." Nadia points to Maximus. "It's his nickname/stage name. We'll go down to his studio later on."

Mash uncovers Cassia and lifts her in his arms.

"We're going to put these bags up and give you two a moment to get acquainted," I say, looking at Launa for approval. "Unless you want to call it a night?"

Launa sips from her glass. "I'm good right now. I'll come find you after I finish my drink."

Chapter 10

London

Launa

I SECRETLY TAKE IN THE BEAUTY OF THE mansion while Nadia and I make small talk. The impromptu trip to London was already over the top, but staying the night in the biggest house I've ever stepped foot in has thrown me off of my game. I'm beyond wowed.

The ceilings are high enough to fit my parents' house in the open space. The color scheme in the front room is eggshell white and beige with pops of royal violet and splashes of red. It reeks of hundred dollar perfumed candles sold at snooty retail stores, and the energy inside transfers a sense of calm and peace over me.

Our hosts, a fine-ass white boy and a *sistah* with the smoothest dark skin to make a dermatologist proud, appear to be crazy about Levi. I contemplate which questions to ask her about him, but get distracted by the expensive fragrance she wears that brings me back to her luminous skin. The question, 'What's your *secret?'* is on the tip of my tongue when I convince myself to wait until we've gotten to know each other a little better—even though I know the answer is money.

She greets me in her rich-woman getup—a cropped two-piece exercise outfit with a cashmere cardigan draped around her shoulders. I peg her to be bougie like Landon, who wears similar getups when she works out, and I giggle to myself that God has a sense of humor, sending me to spend the rest of my holiday with another version of my sister.

The Lululemon Twins, I kid to myself.

Nadia pulls me from talking shit about her in my head. "Levi tells me you're from Charlotte. How have you managed living so far away from home?"

"It wasn't easy at first, but love made it so."

"Love, huh? Can't say I've ever experienced a love that profound."

Nadia snickers behind her glass. "You and I both know that isn't true," she adds, twirling the ends of her long black hair with her fingers.

"What makes you say something like that without even knowing me? I mean we just met."

"I know the look of love when I see it. And I know Levi. He's like a second brother to me. He's feeling you."

I sip to hide my blushing cheeks. "I'm enjoying his company, but I don't throw the L word around. Like I said, I've never felt it before. My track record of picking the wrong guys to get entangled with is impeccable."

She reaches her glass forward to tap mine. "I make money telling such stories."

"Well, I have zero interest in telling mine. I'd pay for a refresh. I would get it right if I had the chance."

"I'd say you've got it right this time."

Nadia glares at me between an awkward lull. The kids can be heard laughing and playing instead of going to sleep, and she sighs.

"This house belongs in magazines. I don't think I've ever been in a more beautiful home, but if you ever meet my sister, I will deny saying that."

Nadia laughs. "Years ago, I would have given Mash all the credit since he is the big star on this side of the world, but after popping out two kids and making a little change myself, I'm going to say thank you. So, you have a sister?"

"I do."

"I always wanted a sister. I have a hard-headed brother instead. My girlfriends back home fill that void as much as they can—a few of them at least."

"I know what you mean. I had a friend who felt like a sister, but..." I catch myself getting too personal and take a longer sip to fix my mistake.

"But..."

Fuck

"But we haven't spoken in a while."

She places her glass on an engraved black-coated wooden coaster. *The Sharpers,* it reads in rose-gold ink. At the foot of the sofa rests a gray suede ottoman. She lifts the top and pulls out a photo album.

Talking to herself while scanning the pages in search of a photograph, I can tell she is dying to talk about her life back in the States. Her eyes light up as the memories flip in front of her.

I bite my tongue and ask, "How bad do you long for your old life?"

Her focus during her search causes her not to hear me. "Here it is." She lays the book in my lap. "That's my squad. We haven't all been to-gether since Shannon's wedding five years ago." She points to the bride in the middle. "But that'll all change this summer. We have a mini reunion planned during my husband's summer residency in Spain. You and Levi will be our first house guests when we fly out tomorrow night."

My eyes widen. "Spain?"

"Yes. Have you been?"

My face flushes from lack of living. "This is the first time I have left the U.S."

She gasps.

I panic that she is about to belittle me, and I'm going to have to check her in her own house. I narrow my eyes at her as a warning.

She taps my knee. "I was the same way when I first came here."

"Really?" I exhale.

"Yes. Except, as you can see, I ended up staying. Not at first, but you get the picture."

She peers at the hallway, then whispers, "This is Levi's ex." Her eyes roll, then she points to Taylor's picture. "We'll talk about her more when we're truly alone."

"About that...Levi didn't mention we were going to Spain on this trip."

She covers her mouth. "Shit. Don't tell him you know. He was probably going to surprise you."

"He surprised me with the tickets here already. Is he always like this?"

Nadia glances back over to the hallway. "What's it been, a week, since you two met?"

I nod.

"Since the divorce, Levi has traveled with us on several excursions. He's met women wherever we went, but he's never brought one to our home or invited anyone to travel with us." She closes the book. "Do with that as you will."

My fingers toy with the necklace he gave me for Christmas. "So what's in Spain?"

"The hubs was asked to spin at some hot nightclub to bring in the new year. The four of us will be there for two days. I promise we'll have a good time."

Chapter 11

Spain

Levi

WE LAND IN IBIZA, AND I CAN'T READ Launa. She hides behind oversized sunglasses covering the top half of her face and pinching her nose. If she's excited to be here, I can't tell right off, and I wonder if I'm making a mistake in bringing her on this trip—because this life isn't mine. I don't have access to private jets and family friends who house planes in their backyard. My friends have these connections. I hope she understands this.

The house we arrive to is in a gated community hidden in the hills overlooking the calm, turquoise ocean. Nadia stares at a huge rock she's fascinated with from the balcony, telling Launa facts about its powers and how she believes it possesses the power of love—a story she's told me a thousand times before.

Launa glances over at me as she listens to Nadia rave on. Deep down, I hope love is on her mind when she looks at me. I've been feeling it for her since the moment we met, but blerds like me can't risk telling the cool girl that too early.

Mash calls for me to come with him to the club. I take one final look at Launa and wave goodbye. She smiles at me, and Nadia turns around.

"I'm sorry. Let me give you two a moment alone before you leave."

I thank Nadia and ease behind her. My hand caresses Launa's waist before locking in front of her. With my chin resting on her shoulder, I embrace the silence between us and close my eyes to appreciate the moment. A light flash of wind envelopes around us, and I hold her even tighter.

"Everything okay? You've been quiet since we boarded the plane."

Her hand covers mine. "I'm cool."

"I said I wasn't going to mention this, but I'm curious. Is this all too much?"

She looks at me over her shoulder. "Now you ask me this?"

I gulp at her honesty, then she laughs. "Of course it's too much, but I'm enjoying myself. You didn't have to keep this a secret from me. I would have been excited to come here all the same."

"Whew!" I sigh and kiss her cheek. "You had me scared I fucked up for a second."

She chuckles. "We're good."

"I promise we'll be better than good later

on tonight. Do you mind if I run with Mash to the club?"

"Go enjoy your bromance."

I crack up and turn her loose. "So, Nadia told you about that, huh?"

"She did, and she didn't lie." She leans back, and I kiss her lips. "Go enjoy yourself. I'm hitting it off with Nadia. I'll be fine."

At the club, I feel in the way until Mash introduces me to his assistant, Gemma. She leads me to the VIP section overlooking the crowd behind the deejay booth. The club is closed, but the staff offers me drinks and food while I wait for Mash to finish tying up loose ends.

When he joins me, I'm three beers in and nearly full off of appetizers.

"I didn't bring you here to party by yourself. Sorry that took so long. I wanted us to get a chance to catch up before you get stuck with the ladies when the chaos starts."

Our beers chime when we tap bottles.

"It's good to see you happy, mate. Told you not to give up on love."

"Love?" I question him.

"Don't try to deny it, yeah. I've seen you with many birds over the years. She's no bird."

"You can say that." I lower my head. "I don't want to lose this one, man. How could I have fallen for her in one week?"

Mash raises a brow. "The pot says to the kettle." He snickers. "I knew it when I saw Nadia under those strobe lights."

"So, I'm not crazy?"

"When it happens, there's nothing you can do about it, yeah. Except hope you don't fuck it up."

Chapter 12

New Year's

Launa

I'm on a whirlwind vacation with a man I hardly know, but somehow it feels like I've been waiting on him all this time. And it frightens me. When something's too good to be true, it usually is, but when I look at Levi, I hope for my sake he proves that old saying wrong.

Nadia seems to be a good friend, but she's not completely honest. Motherhood is weighing heavy on her, and she won't admit it. I listen to the cracks between her upbeat chats, but from one mother to another, I know that shit is hard. I know she needed this break.

I ask her. "When is the last time you took a day just for yourself?"

She turns pensive. "I...I can't remember when. It's either family trips, work trips, the husband's work trips, or trips back home."

"So, it's been a while?"

"Does hanging out with a friend count?"

"No. Just you."

"Then that would be years—and during a tumultuous time. Is that something you do?"

I grin. "I drop my son off with my mother, then I either lock myself in the house and run through all the snacks, watch movies that make me cry, read a book from cover to cover, or fly out of town someplace I've never been. I'll usually tour whatever city I wind up in, eat an expensive meal, drink myself to sleep, then come back home refreshed. I highly recommend it."

"Sounds like it. I'll keep that in mind."

"This is gonna sound weird, but what would it take to charter a plane?"

"Not much, from what I know, but the pilot who flew us here is a family friend. May I ask why?"

"You know historical facts about this place. Are you familiar with these?" I show her the screenshots in my phone of the places we received postcards from, then lie. "When I learned we were going to Spain, I told my sister, and she recommended I visit these places. I was wondering what it would cost, the protocols, the planning. That sort of thing."

She skims them carefully with a questionable brow. "We can probably visit these two tomorrow. They're like an hour and a half away," she says of Barcelona and Mallorca. "Mr. Hunt's taken us there before, but this place is new to me." She points to the picture of the first destination we received a card from, San Sebastián. "I'll tell Mr. Hunt our plans, and you

84

and I will make it a day of shopping and gossip."

♫

Nadia and I cackle when we meet in the living room both dressed in sequin mini dresses.

"If we had on the same color I would just die." She laughs. "Great minds think alike."

"Coming from you, an obvious fashionista, I'll take the compliment."

The streets of Ibiza are crowded beyond measure. I get a taste of A-list celebrity life being in the company of Levi's friends. Lines don't exist. Stares are never-ending *and* worrisome, and money flows freely, so I hide my wealth and go along with the flow.

High above the stage, we watch a crowd wave fluorescent bands and phone lights as they party clunked together like wet sugar. I look around and feel important, also overly anxious at the people below staring up at us—or rather me, trying to figure out who I am and what level of importance I belong in.

Levi's breath warms the back of my shoulder. He's holding me tight, grinding his rock-hard dick between my ass cheeks to a techno song. Nothing about this music warrants him to poke me in the ass or dance so intimate and close.

"I can't wait 'til we get back to the house."

"Are you sure you can last that long?" I tease him.

"Are you suggesting what I think you're suggesting?"

I look back at him. "Down, boy. I ain't going to jail in this strange country where I don't speak the language and don't know the customs." I kiss my teeth. "These people won't snatch me up for public lewdness."

"I'd risk it—for you."

"Of course you would. You don't have a pussy."

He backs up, turns me around, and dances with me in front of the other VIPs in the booth. Nadia raises a glass to us, and I blush. Not only because all eyes are on us, but I'm also turned on that Levi doesn't hide how he feels for me, and his bulge refuses to fall back.

Mash calls for Nadia and all his special guests in the booth to join him onstage. As everyone heads down the stairs and fills the elevator, I find myself living in the moment.

"Let's stay up here," I suggest.

"You sure?"

I tell him yes with an enticing gaze.

With champagne glasses in our hands, we stand at the edge of the balcony. I hike my skirt up just enough that I can spread my legs and place Levi's free hand on my bared hips.

He grunts in my ear. "Does this mean you've changed your mind?"

I nod.

"Oooh, baby," he whines, placing his glass on the banister.

Mash and Nadia look up at us from the

stage. I wave at them as Levi slides my panties to the left, smiling over my shoulder. When he raises my ass up and spreads my cheeks wide, he falls to his knees, and I'm pushed to stand on tipped toes.

"Uh," I sigh below the music from his wavering tongue lubing me in front of thousands. I squeeze the stem of my glass so hard I catch myself before it breaks, then grip onto the railing for balance.

Struggling not to close my eyes, I focus on the television screens above the bar behind the dance floor, petrified we'll be caught, but can't stop my urge to live dangerously in the moment. I want him.

Two fingers slip inside my slit and shake up the wetness he's drawn from my fountain. He rises upright, unfastens his zipper, then slides inside me so smoothly I don't jolt.

We fake as if we're dancing to the music, fucking each other off beat. He whines in my ear. Sighing. Lips trembling.

"Fuck, baby," he says below his breath. "Bless you for not making me wait for this pussy I have missed so much. I fucking love you, girl."

I hold myself from saying "I love you, too." Stunned that I want to say it at all.

Mash begins to countdown from ten over the speakers, and Levi grips me tighter. His dick swells a tad more and feels sturdier on each sneaky stroke.

"Seven, six, five..." I gasp, reaching back to

T.K. RICHARDS

caress the back of his neck while I come on his dick.

"Three, two, one," he whispers, then stiffens inside of me. "Ahhh," he grunts, turning my head to kiss him. "Happy New Year, baby," he says, then tongues me at midnight.

I carry his mess in my panties when half of the crowd exits the club to watch the fireworks light up the black sky. Nadia returns with Mash to the balcony, popping a fresh bottle of bubbly in his hand.

"Happy New Year!" Mash pours the rich-people champagne into four glasses.

Nadia passes one to each of us. "Happy New Year!" She comes in for a hug.

"This is a special bottle I had reserved just for us," Mash says. "To friends."

We raise our glasses.

"To family." Nadia looks at Levi, then me.

"To love," Levi adds, pulling me in close.

"To love," I say, looking deep into his eyes.

Chapter 13

Tourists

Launa

AN EARLY MORNING SESSION OF TAKE THE dick and give him a lick, to celebrate the exchanging of eight letters I've never said before, eased the blow to Levi's ego that he was not invited to travel with me and Nadia.

He reminds me, "They say the way you bring in the new year is what you'll do for the next 364 days."

"That sounds like a lot of sex, my friend. Let's make sure it comes with passion."

"That I can promise."

Nadia and I fly into the open blue sky but don't talk much once we're levitated. It's not until Mr. Hunt reminds us to buckle up for landing in Mallorca, an hour later, that she looks up from her phone, and I look up from my book.

I pretend to be interested in what she's teaching me about the sites as if she's a paid tour guide. She thinks I'm curious, the way my eyes are roaming like the winding second hand on a clock, clueless that I'm studying the faces of people walking by in hopes I'll see Jen.

The more she teaches me about history, the more she reminds me of Landon—knowledgeable about shit no one else cares about.

I laugh to myself, thinking of yesterday and how her face lit up when talking about that rock, Es Vedra. I don't believe for one second it holds magical powers, but I wouldn't say that to someone being overly kind to me. And I definitely won't tell her I said I love you to Levi. She'll give that rock credit for me falling in love.

"Look." She points to hot air balloons sailing across the sky. "Would you get on one of those?"

"Not for money, or a dare."

She pulls out her phone and takes a picture of us with the balloons in the background. "Mash is adventurous. He convinced me to let go of my fears and go up once."

"You must really love him, because I would never."

"You can say that! It was beautiful up there, but definitely not happening again." She shakes her head. "Most people who come here visit the secret coves, but that's something you should experience with your man, not me. Speaking of your man, how was bringing in the new year with him?"

I study the smirk on her face, wondering if Levi blabbed about what we did in the club to her husband, and if he in turn blabbed to her during pillow talk. But I don't confess.

"It was better than I expected. I blame it on the vacation. It brings out a different, adventurous side of me."

"Mm-hmm," she moans.

Dammit. She knows.

"I'm gonna have to bring myself back down to earth when I get home. You know...remind myself I'm not famous and that this isn't my life."

"But it could be." Her voice says with sincerity.

"What do you mean?"

"Levi and Mash are really close if you haven't noticed. He's been the third wheel to many events we've attended. And if he's with someone, that invitation extends to her."

"Cool." I purse my lips. "That's sweet to have friends that love you like that. You're making me miss my rowdy bunch."

♡

We share a trio of street tacos and a box of classic ensaïmadas. The powerful flavors bring us a second round of quiet time between us. Between her moaning at the sugary croissant-like pastry and my lips smacking of fresh onions and pork dripping from the homemade shell, we snicker at each other when we're done.

She looks at her watch. "If we want to visit Barcelona, we ought to get going and visit the place your sister recommended." She smiles as she gathers her leftovers.

"What's that look for?" I ask her.

She blushes. "Barcelona is where I got married. I haven't been back in a while. You're gonna love it."

The hour spent back in the air is chatty this time. Nadia asks more questions about my life back home. I keep the conversation on family, and distract her from digging deeper with a re-direct on the gossip she promised me about Levi's ex.

My mouth drops open when she tells me of the ordeal from beginning to end.

"So what I'm hearing is he married a nasty bitch, and I have no reason to worry about this girl."

"Not at all."

I do a double-take at Nadia.

She chortles. "You reminded me of my girl-friend Shannon just now."

"How so?"

"I heard how I sounded, and she's quick to call out when a British accent slips out of me."

"Not at all," I mock her.

Nadia keels over in laughter.

I try again. "Not at all. I can't say it like you."

She catches her breath and forces herself to say it with the accent again. "Not...it's like re-moving the a in at, then connect the t's together."

"Nottall," I say.

"You got it!"

Mr. Hunt laughs at us and tells us to secure for landing once again.

A car service drives us around this time. The first stop in Barcelona is to a street vendor selling tapas.

"I know we ate an hour ago, but I have to see if they taste like I remember." She bites it with her eyes closed. Her head begins to nod, then she licks her lips. "The next time you and Levi come to visit, we're going to spend a few days here. There's so much to take in, you can't get the feel of how special this place is in a day."

"Deal," I say, then order what she's having.

We finish our second lunch during a stroll to a small market close to the beach entrance. She tells me this is where she was married and buys a wire ring from a man who pretends he remembers her.

Once the visit has stopped being about her, she orders the driver to take us to see the most beautiful architectural buildings in the world. The colors, design, features, and creativity are so out of this world, I can't imagine another place exists that compares. I say this to Nadia.

She responds, "You may be right. Of course, Dubai is a site to see, but I agree with your take about this place. It truly is something special."

We roam to the most famous street in the city, La Rambla. Down narrow streets, we pose for pictures in front of historical churches, gothic-inspired rooftops on homes, and blend in with the other tourists for over an hour.

"Mr. Hunt will be calling us back soon. Let's find your stop, then head back."

I look at the street sign. "Actually, we're on the street of the art exhibit I'd like to see...Arts Santa Monica."

"Did you plug it in your phone?"

"I accidentally left my phone back at the house."

Nadia scowls. "I guess everyone is glued to these things except you, huh? I'll look up the address."

A weird silence lulls between us as I follow her toward the exhibit building. We're met with the tapping noise of a live show in action—a ginger-haired woman chiseling a figure out of ice in front has drawn a patient crowd waiting to witness her sculpture in its final form.

Yards away stands a crowd admiring a mural created by a local artist. Their whispers of opinions and interpretations travel around the space like echoes of an invisible wind.

A dark exhibit takes place down the other stretch of the open floor where a short, black-haired man is in the process of a light installation in its first phase. I search through the many faces in attendance, some masked, some exposed, and still no sight of Jen.

We walk through arched doorways and encounter a wall mural of artwork. Some painted, some penciled, and many variations of colors and techniques for a diverse presentation.

I gasp. "Max."

"What'd you just say?" Nadia's voice heightens in confusion.

My eyes fixate on a black-and-white picture of a boy with Max's face, and tears form in my eyes. "Max," I say, then smile.

Nadia grabs my arm. "Why are you calling my husband's name?"

"Excuse me for a moment." I walk away in search of a curator.

Frantically, I search the building with Nadia pressing on my heels. I bump into a woman covered in paint with a lanyard hanging from her neck.

"Do you work here?" I ask.

"No anglais," she says.

I turn to Nadia. "Do you speak Spanish?"

Her eyes widen. "I'd like an answer to my question first."

I exhale deeply as I dig in my purse and show the woman Jen's picture. She shakes her head incessantly and points in the direction behind her.

Nadia follows me down a short hallway where an office sits in the corner.

"Are you in charge here?" I ask a woman dressed in a beige sheath dress.

She looks up at me through tinted oval glasses, her hair up in a bun with a pen sticking out of one end, and a wooden accessory out of the other. Her English is broken, but she delivers an answer in the most beautiful of combined accents.

"I am."

"I'd like to buy a piece from your mural."

"We create here. No sell."

"I may not look like it, but I can pay you whatever you want."

"Miss, I don't know what to tell you."

"Can I show you the one I'm interested in?"

"I'd be happy to give you information on a piece, but I cannot sell you an artist's work."

She sighs and pushes her glasses up her nose. I speed back to the wall with her heels clacking on the floor. Nadia's face is stuck in a panic mode, walking beside her. I glance in her direction and am met with a look of regret and confusion.

"I'd love it if you could change your rules this one time and sell me that piece." I point to Max's portrait.

The curator squints. "I'm sorry. That work was donated."

"What if I donate money to you in its place? How much do you think it's worth?"

Nadia butts in. "What is so important about this picture? And I still would like to know why you called my husband's name."

"I didn't. I called *his* name." I dig in my purse and scoff. "Ugh. If I had my phone, I could show you his picture." I open my card holder and pull out Jen's picture. I ask the curator, "Have you seen this woman before?"

Her eyes grow big and wide behind the

lens. "I...don't know. If you'll excuse me please."

Nadia stares at the photograph over my shoulder and sternly whispers, "With all due respect, Launa, what the fuck is going on?"

I show her Jen's picture. "The friend I told you I haven't seen in a while...this is her. And that picture is identical to her son, Max. The son I am helping raise now that she's gone."

Her chest sinks, and her lips part. Her eyes lose their growing rage and turn soft when they look at me. I take a deep breath to settle my nerves and look around for the curator.

"Where did that lady run off to?"

"I don't know." Nadia looks for her as well. "Tell you what, I can offer her top dollar and see if she is willing to part with the portrait, then I think it's best we start to head back to the plane."

"Thank you. I appreciate the offer, but I can manage."

Her hands rise above her shoulders. "I was just trying to help."

I place my hand on her arm. "You have. You got me here. I'll explain more when we get on the plane."

A tap on the shoulder from the curator surprises me. "Follow me back to my office, please."

Nadia checks the time as we stroll behind. My heart races with hope the arts center will part with the portrait that could possibly hold a clue. We step inside, and the curator slips me a note.

She smiles. "Good luck. Be sure you are not followed."

2

Nadia asks to see Jen's picture during the drive to the address. She scowls at it for a few seconds, mumbling inaudibly to herself.

She snaps a copy of it with her phone. "I recognize this face."

"Maybe you saw coverage of her disappearance on the news," I suggest.

"No, that's not it."

The five-minute drive leads us to a colorful, underground neighborhood. Nadia clutches her purse, and I chuckle.

"You can stay in the car. I should be fine."

"I'm a mother. My kids come first and need me, and I didn't ask to be a part of whatever this is you've got going on."

"I totally understand." I give her a hug. "Thank you, Nadia. If I'm not back in ten minutes, I won't expect you to still be here."

She sighs and snaps my picture.

"Why'd you do that?"

"In case I have to describe to the cops what you were last seen wearing." She squeezes my hand when I open the door. "Good luck, like that lady said."

I step out onto the dark, narrow street, embracing fear of what or who I will find, and pray to myself Nadia has a heart and won't leave me behind.

A man smoking a cigar whistles at me while a young kid holds the door to the building open for me. I keep my eyes straight, making zero contact with anyone I cross.

I pass women carrying groceries and teenage girls laughing at me as I climb two flights of stairs. An elderly woman meets me at the top of the second floor, looks me up and down, and says something in Spanish I can't make out. She points to the number on the note —215. I grow nervous that she knows why I am in the building.

I knock. The door opens, and I hold my breath. A brown woman scolds me with her eyes, blows out a cloud of smoke on the side of her mouth, then smiles.

"Por aquí." She steps outside, walks two doors down, and beats on the door with her inner wrist.

The door swings wide, and tears swell in my eyes at the sight of Jen looking back at me. She pulls me inside a barren apartment with a calendar centered on dark-mustard walls, and a chaise positioned by the balcony door.

My eyes find it hard to ignore the bed sheets blowing against the window on a line as she holds me so tight I feel our hearts beat against each other.

I can barely breathe, and my voice cracks when I call her name. "Jen. I can't believe I found you."

"I've been waiting for one of you to figure out it was me," she says.

I pull back and grab her face. "You won't believe how I got here. And I don't have much time." I hug her again.

"How is my boy?" she asks.

"I wish I had a picture of him with me. I didn't risk bringing my phone in case I was being tracked."

"Ugh, I'd give anything to see him." Tears fall on her cheeks. "To hold him."

"There is a photo of him on the school's website. He and Tim are on the football team. You remember which school is in his district?"

"I do."

"Jen, I quit my job and sub at the school to watch over both our boys. I'm keeping my promise to you."

"I knew you and Landon would. How is she?"

"I wish I had more time to tell you her drama, but she's great. She's a mother of two. Can you believe that?"

Jen keels over in tears. "No! I cannot. God, I'm missing so much."

My chest caves as I join her, bawling like melting ice. She holds my hands as our foreheads touch.

"I need you to stay sharp, Launa."

"I will."

"I move around every six months."

"When is your next move? We have to do something about this. You can't keep this up.

Do you need money? How would I get it to you?"

"I'm fine." She mouths and widens her eyes. "I make do working at a nightclub down the street—getting paid under the table."

"I don't wanna leave you here."

She sniffles and wipes her eyes. "You have to. But I will let you know I'm okay."

"I'll be paying close attention." Our hands release. "I'm gonna leave you with this...Jay and Millicent...done deal. He said he was gonna commit but flaked."

Jen bursts into laughter. "Of course he did."

"I think he misses you."

"He should." She hugs me a final time. "Tell him I miss his toxic ass, too. Just not in that way."

I giggle. "I will."

I look at her neighbor guarding the door and work my way over. Jen stays in the middle of the room with her hands pressed to her chest.

"I love you, sis," I say and wave goodbye.

Locks sound off behind me as the neighbor escorts me outside. The red brake lights of the car light up my silhouette as I scoot to the back door. I tap on the window, hop inside when it unlocks, and look back at the building until we turn the corner.

Nadia hands me a tissue. I cry into it like a baby until it's soaked. She hands me a second sheet and wraps her arm around me. I need her consoling and support as I fail to pull myself together.

The flight back to Ibiza is silent. I promised Nadia I would tell her the story, but she doesn't ask, and I have no voice to tell it. The most I'm able to say to her is, "Thank you," when the plane lands us safely on the island.

She sits with me for a moment before we exit the plane, and join Mash and Levi waiting for us by the car. I slide my sunglasses on before Levi approaches.

Mr. Hunt hands me off to him. "Have a lovely evening, ma'am."

"Thanks for bringing the girls back safe, Mr. Hunt." Levi nods at him and wraps his arms around me. "Shades at night? You two must have had a good time."

I squeeze his hand and bow my head as he escorts me to the car. Nadia hides her face in Maximus's chest.

"You good, babe?" he asks her.

She snuggles further into him. "I'm happy to see you. I missed you. And I'm ready to get back to my babies."

"We will. Levi and I planned a couple's spa day tomorrow before we depart. Thought you two would enjoy that after the long day you've had."

"They seem tired out, don't they?" Levi leans into me. "You good?"

I nod. "Tired, like you said."

I wash the emotions from my face as best I can. Levi sighs when I throw on pajamas after a hot shower. I curl up to him resting on a stack of pillows.

He wraps his arms around me. "You that tired?"

I rest my feet next to his. "Long day."

"You and Nadia were pretty quiet on the way home. You two didn't say a word to each other."

"She's cool. Travel has worn me out is all."

"That's why we scheduled a day of pampering for tomorrow.

"Levi, thank you. For everything. Especially this trip."

He squeezes me and kisses my forehead. "You did say you love me."

I give him the tenderest of kisses. "I do," I say.

I really, really do.

Chapter 14

We've Only Just Begun

Levi

I WAKE TO AN EMPTY BED, FEELING FOR THE warm body dancing in my dreams. I stretch and take in fresh air from the balcony, surprised Launa isn't looking out at the ocean.

The smell of bacon and eggs hits my nose, putting extra pep in my step to hurry to the kitchen. I'm taken aback that Launa isn't at the breakfast bar with Nadia and Mash.

My brows furrow from the look on their faces when I join them. "Good morning."

Nadia avoids eye contact with me. "Mornin'."

"Where's Launa?"

Mash takes a deep sigh. "Did you two chat a bit last night?"

"Chat? About what?"

He looks at Nadia and huffs. "She left before daylight, brother."

"Left?"

"Tell him," Mash says to Nadia.

My hands run across my face and pause

over my mouth. I breathe into my palms, staring at the walls as the room begins to turn black.

"Did she say anything before she left?"

"Just to tell you that she loves you and she's sorry."

"Sorry about what? We were having a great fucking time. She was different when you two came back last night." I point at Nadia. "Just what the fuck happened yesterday?"

Mash stands up from the counter. "I know you're upset, and you're my good mate, but I won't allow you to talk to my wife like—"

"It's okay," Nadia interrupts. "He doesn't mean it." She gestures for me to sit.

"She's right. I don't mean to disrespect either of you. Sorry about that. I just don't understand."

"Something did happen yesterday, and I'm guessing she left before I could tell you."

♡

I take a shot for breakfast when I learn of the wild goose chase Launa led Nadia on. I feel foolish for not knowing what was going on. Foolish for falling so fast. Foolish for bringing her around the people I love, only to embarrass myself.

"Are you sure she's a school teacher?" Nadia asks.

"Yeah. Why?"

"Well, yesterday she was willing to pay top

dollar for that portrait, and to fly out of here at the last minute is pretty steep."

I lose my mind in the moment. "You two won't mind if I cancel our plans and hang back here?"

"Not at all."

I call Launa incessantly. No answer. I text her. No reply. And by the time the sky is no longer blue and my best friends return from the day we planned together, I find myself boarding the jet alone, left on read, holding onto so many words unsaid.

Chapter 15

And This Is Why I Don't

Launa

I HIDE MY SWOLLEN EYES BEHIND ROUND sunglasses as I wait near the sliding doors for over an hour. Travelers walking past annoy me with their stares, as if they have to know why a woman traveling solo has on shades when the moon is out.

"You wanna talk about it?" Landon asks over the speaker once Todd has arrived.

"I will when I get there. Make sure the babies are fast asleep."

Levi's name lights up my phone screen.

Todd sighs. "You could let him know you arrived safely."

"I didn't let him know I was leaving."

"That man is probably going crazy." He looks at me with a raised brow before he takes off. "Not unless... Am I gonna have to fuck ol' boy up?"

I smile for the first time in hours. "No. This one was all on me."

Todd scoffs. "I can't wait to hear this one."

Landon opens the door and hugs me when I walk in. I hold her tight, and she pulls back to read my eyes.

"I was worried when you called, but in looking at you, I'm even more worried now. What happened?"

I point to the kitchen, and she follows me. I write on a notepad: *Grab your coat and leave your phone inside.* Landon scowls and shows it to Todd. He sighs and rechecks the locks on the house, places his phone on the counter, and holds Landon's hand as they follow me closer to the waves.

Landon bounces from the chilling winds blowing around us. "I thought we were done with these kinds of meetings."

"Will we ever be?" I respond.

"So what happened with him to warrant us freezing our asses off in the middle of the night?"

"I've been keeping secrets from everyone."

Landon's eyes grow big.

"Since our lives were turned upside down, I noticed junk mail coming from different parts of Spain being delivered to us."

"Who is us?" Todd asks.

I point to Landon. "It was in her mail when she first moved down here. In mine. And in Jay's. I didn't say anything because I didn't want to get anyone worked up over a theory I've been wrestling with. But now, it's no longer a theory. Jen is alive."

The shudders between the two of them

pause. They stare at me in disbelief. Landon's mouth parts open to speak, but nothing comes out. Todd squeezes her waist as he studies my face.

"People have doppelgängers, La. Maybe you think you saw someone who looks like her."

"No, it was her. I hugged her. We talked. We cried. She was shocked to hear you two have children. We laughed about Jay and Millicent. Then, she broke down because she misses Max terribly. She misses all of us."

Landon shakes her head. "What *was* your theory exactly?"

"She was sending us signals that she was okay. Before she left the country with Jules, she promised me to secrecy about plans she had in place to free Max of any revenge surrounding the money. She was prepared not to come back to the States."

Landon's eyes lit up. "So that's why you moved into my house to sub at the school."

"Yes. I promised to take care of Max for her. She knew Jay and Millicent would eventually fizzle out, and wanted to make sure he would be okay when it happened."

Landon hugs me. "I can't imagine what it was like keeping this to yourself. I'm proud of you, Launa."

I embrace her and exhale. "It feels good to finally share all of this with you."

"Well, how is she? How does she look? Where is she? Is she safe?"

"She looks good. She's lost weight. She

moves around a lot, hence the different post cards. And right now, she's laying low in Spain."

Landon frowns. "I thought your trip was to London?"

"Turns out Levi's friends are loaded. They have private jets and shit, and they flew us to Ibiza for a show."

Todd chuckles as I retell how I convinced Nadia to take a day trip without the husbands. Landon's eyes never leave me until I mention the portrait of Max hanging on the wall at the exhibit. She lays her head on Todd's shoulder and holds him close when I get to the part about Jen standing on the opposite side of the second apartment door.

"So what do we do now?"

"I barely had five minutes with her. All we can do is keep our eyes and ears open for where she will be next."

Todd looks up at the house. "Let's head back inside. But before we do, I have a million-dollar question—do we tell Jay or not?"

I shrug my shoulders. "That's something we three need to decide."

"What about ol' boy?"

"I got scared. What are the odds Levi would take me to Spain—the very place where Jen was hiding?"

"But not to the exact location," Landon argues.

"Still, it feels very strange. *And* he's an investigator."

114

Her big sister mode kicks in and she quizzes me. "So you don't trust him?"

"It's quite the opposite. I do trust him. He's breaking down walls I need to stand in order to protect myself. I wanted to tell him everything after knowing him for what— a week! What is that?"

Todd bows his head. "Now I understand why you ran."

"So do I," Landon smiles at me. "You're in love."

I sniffle and catch the tear spilling over from one of my eyes. Landon squeezes my hand, and another tear flies in the wind before it falls in the sand.

"It's better to end it this way before we get too deep," I say.

Landon looks at Todd, then back at me. "I think you've already crossed that line."

Chapter 16

Ain't No Sunshine

Levi

I FLY BACK TO THE STATES WITH EGG ON MY face, my tail tucked, and my heart in shambles. If I could open a window on the plane, I'd rip my shattered heart from my chest to stop the internal bleeding and throw it in the Atlantic.

'I quit,' I tell myself. *'Fuckboys don't get their heart broken like this.'*

I say this to myself as Launa ignores my call for the fiftieth time. Making me look like a stalker. Feel like a desperate simp. Turn me into a pussy-whipped joke.

I avoid looking at myself in the mirror for days. The anger and hurt I feel is evident for weeks while I handle the lawsuit for my family's property. I show no mercy toward the land developers, and deny our attorney to counter any negotiations outside of drop their false claims, or be met with a harassment countersuit.

My grandfather is proud at how vicious I come across in the courtroom.

"I knew I was leaving all of this in the right hands," he tells me.

"I'm not so sure about that, Daddy. I don't think any children of my own will be running around in this yard unfortunately."

"Is that what's going on witchu?"

I lower my head.

"What happened?"

"That's just it. I wish I knew. And it doesn't look like I ever will. She won't take my calls. It's been weeks and no word from her. I've been ghosted."

He pats my shoulder. "Son, relationships are wonderful. *They not* easy, but I wouldn't have enjoyed my life without all the turmoil, the ups and downs, or the highs and lows if I had to do it all alone. Going at it with a partner makes life worth it. Is she worth it?"

"I thought so."

"These electronics have taken the romance out of relationships. Go to her. You have to hold her hand, and look her in her eyes, and speak from your heart. Not type your feelings in a text chat—or whatever it is you young people do."

I laugh. "I really want to, but..."

"But nothing. You either fight for her, or let the next man have the life you want to live."

♡

To celebrate that the courtroom battle, my family pours in to cook a feast. The attention and praise becomes too much for me to bear, so I slip out of the house and take a drive around the island to clear my head—also, to air out the jealousy that I don't have anyone on my side, like my other cousins, to share the moment with.

My grandfather's words ring in my head the closer I drive toward the beach. I muster up the courage to knock on Todd and Landon's door just shy of the sun sinking into the ocean with Launa's name on the tip of my tongue.

Todd answers the door. "Bruh, it's Valentine's night. Are you serious right now?" he mumbles on the side of his mouth and widens his eyes. "We just put our kids to bed."

"Who is that?" Landon asks in the background.

Todd steps aside and opens the door wider.

"Oh," she says. "Let him in."

Todd whispers, "Make it fast, man. I know you feel me right now." He shakes my hand. "How's it going?"

"It could be better, but I'm not gonna complain. Thought I would swing by and have a word with you two before I head out of town."

"Hope that means you came through for your people?"

"Finalized everything earlier today."

"That's what's up, man." Todd shakes my hand again.

"Yeah, one obstacle down." I sigh. "Which brings me here."

"Launa," he says.

I nod. "I don't know where things went wrong...where I went wrong. I came here hoping you could provide me some insight."

"Please, have a seat." Landon sits first. "You did nothing wrong to my knowledge."

"That's good to know because Launa will not return the *fiftyleven* calls I've made to her."

"What did your friend in London say to you about their trip?"

"All I know is something peculiar happened about a portrait. They went to a colorful neighborhood, then Launa went into a building and came out crying. She wasn't the same when they came back, and she left in the middle of the night without saying goodbye." I take a deep breath. "I need closure. Nothing is owed to me, but I need it. I was hoping one of you could tell me something."

"Is closure really what you want?" Landon asks me, and I hold my breath.

Todd eyes me as a warning to think about the question and to answer it carefully. Landon inches forward to the edge of her seat while I think how to respond.

I pause, choking between honesty and integrity fighting to be the response that escapes my tongue as curious, eager eyes glare at me.

"No. I don't want closure," I say, as honesty wins the battle. "I want your sister."

Landon looks at Todd, and he chimes in. "That's good to know, because we liked you together."

"I love her, man."

"We can help you, but our help comes with a warning. We'll tell you why my sister flaked, but you'll have to decide here and now if you're going to bail on her, or pursue this relationship." Landon nods at Todd.

He stands. "Let's take a walk, man. Leave your phone on the table."

"It was good seeing you, Landon."

"It was good seeing you, Levi."

"Sorry for interrupting your Valentine's night."

Landon smiles. "It's Valentine's every night in this house. Hopefully, you'll know that feeling soon."

We stroll close to the waves as Todd unloads a history of violence, drama, abuse, murder, cold cases, and ties to a mafia down in the state of Texas.

"Launa doesn't want you to be tied to any of this."

"But it's all in the past. Right?"

"It was, until she saw our friend in Spain. There is always a possibility someone will come looking for Jen, so she disappeared, and we funeralized her. Launa helps raise Jen's son in her absence, and she figured you were too good of a guy to drag into all of this. So she bailed."

"I appreciate her looking out for my best interest. I really do. But I still love her and want to be with her."

"After everything I've just shared with you?"

"Even more. I want to console her for what that guy did to her. I want to be her protector. Her friend. Her man."

"Ahite." Todd gives me dap. "Come back up to the house. My wife may have some ideas on how to win her back. But not for too long."

"I know, I know. It's Valentine's Day."

Chapter 17

Messengers

Launa

OUT OF SIGHT, OUT OF MIND IS A LIE. I wake up with Levi on my mind every morning. I miss his smell lingering in the air, his voice in my ear shelling out compliments, and his smile the moment he sees me walking toward him.

I thought the men I chose to deal with in the past were my biggest mistake, but cutting ties with the first man I have ever truly loved is my greatest.

In losing him, I realize why I've been afraid to love. This hurts worse than any pain I have known in life—after childbirth. The sting lingers day and night and messes up your brain. Love is not ideal when it fails.

The phone calls have become history, and the text messages have stopped. But love letters arrive in the mail every other day. Some short. Some long. Some are poems I assume he copied from a poet. Some of his letters feature lyrics to songs.

I smell them, hoping a whiff of his cologne

will transfer from the page into my nose, feenin' for his scent to light up my day. When they don't, I hold the bland woodsy paper to my chest and remember how good I felt with him on New Year's.

My favorite letter he's written so far says:

"I wish I could build a time machine and go back to the first day I saw you on the beach last Christmas. I would put that week in a bottle and relive it over and over again. I'd get to feel that spark of our first kiss a million times over. See your eyes glimmer in the moonlight while you teach me about the stars, and feel thankful love wasn't done with me yet and revealed the woman I've been waiting for. That week was the best time of my life. I'll cherish it always."

After countless envelopes fill the top drawer of my nightstand, I finally write him back.

"If we'd existed in another time, under different circumstances, we'd be together. I'm sorry that I hurt you and for the way I ended things. You deserve better. I hope you can forgive me."

I regret responding to Levi's last letter as it's been a week with no reply. I hope the last one isn't the final one as I've become accustomed to reading his kind, loving words before I go to bed at night. Especially the letters when he tells me about his day. It makes me feel as though I am right there with him and eases the pain of our distance.

Landon and Todd choose to work with Levi on their move from the island, closer to the coast in Charleston, and Mama and Daddy accept their offer to move into their guesthouse to be closer to the babies. I understand their decision. Babies bring about change.

I have two boys quickly approaching manhood on my hands. They could use the guidance of a real man during their transition, and Jay is not the role model I would choose, but he's all I'm left with.

I hang out at his bar, just outside of Troy, while the boys are next door getting a haircut. Jay strolls in from the back when he's told I'm up front. He flashes a finger at the bartender and plops on the stool next to me.

I ask him. "All of these empty seats and you choose to sit this close to me?"

He brushes my leg in a swift manner. "Girl, you know you want me. Stop frontin'."

Two shot glasses tap the wood in front of us. We toast in silence and gulp the heat like old chums.

"If I move down south with the rest of my family, would you let Max come with me?"

"Hell no, girl. My boy ain't leavin' me."

"He will soon. College is coming up."

Jay grins on the side of his mouth. "You don't want to go down there anyway. You may

127

as well face the facts and look at how fate has thrown us together. You know you want me to scratch that itch ain't nobody else scratchin'." He groans. "Mmm. I know it's good."

"Oh, Jay. You have such a way of swooning a woman. How could I resist not being in the throes of passion when you seduce me with the words of a gentleman like that."

He scratches his head. "You fuckin' with me right now, ain't ya?"

"Yes." I mug his head gently. "Football is big in the south, and both of the boys want to play, so what'd ya say? Todd can step in in your place. So can my Daddy."

"Launa, I would let T show him what I can't, but if something were to happen to my boy, I would never forgive myself. And Jen wouldn't forgive me either."

I shudder at the mention of her name.

Jay studies me. "What's wrong?"

"Nothing. Just thinkin' about how things used to be."

"I catch myself doing a lot of that lately."

I suck my teeth. "*This* from the man who just asked me to bend over because no one is left."

"Nah, it ain't like that. I mean, the offer still stands." He winks at me and grins. "But you know what I was getting at."

"Truth be told, when things didn't work out with you and Millicent, I thought it was because you still love Jen."

"I do. I'll regret fuckin' that up for the rest

of my days. I liked Mills, had a little love for her too, but not like Jen. They both deserved better than me."

"And what, I don't?"

Jay smiles over laughter. "I ain't the settlin' down kind, Lil' Launa. I don't think you are either. We'd be perfect for each other. Jen wasn't happy 'bout the Mills thing, but I think she would give *us* her blessing."

I raise a brow. "Is that right?"

"Just think about it. I mean, you got a son, and I got a son. I say we go half on a baby and shoot for a pretty little girl."

"And that's my cue."

"Your cue for what?"

"To rethink my recent decisions."

Chapter 18

Valuable

Levi

SWEAT FORMS IN MY HANDS AS I ENTER THE Davis home in Flint to begin loading the truck. Launa sits on the couch with her mother, looking like an angel in a thin-strapped ivory dress.

"I was hoping you'd be here," I say.

She gasps, scooting to the edge of her seat. "What are you doing here?" Her mouth stays open as she is shocked to see me.

Mrs. Davis admits, "I asked him to help Todd personally handle *with care* all of my valuables."

"What was wrong with the moving company?"

"What does the word valuable mean, girl." Mrs. Davis clicks her tongue at Launa.

Launa rolls her eyes behind her mother's back. "Come here." She stands and holds out her arms.

I smell her sweet scent before her tiny hands press into my back. I struggle to let her go. But when my dick begins to swell, I pull back and clear my throat.

"Valuables." Launa laughs. "It's probably china made in China, sewing needles, and her magazine collection from back in the day."

I snicker in her ear while struggling to give her space, as the peachy scent I missed overpowers the little restraint I have.

Lingering longer than I should, her fingers slowly release the hem of my shirt. Todd walks in, cheesing like a Cheshire cat, and she takes a step back.

"Are y'all doing a turnaround trip?" Launa's eyes say she hopes the answer is no. "Or are you here for a few days?"

Todd hugs Mrs. Davis. "We're pulling out sometime tomorrow. I'm gonna introduce Levi to the fellas at the bar tonight. You wanna come hang?"

Launa looks at me with the same heat in her eyes as when we were on the dance floor in Hilton Head. "I would, but I don't wanna ruin guys' night out. Go and have a good time." She grabs her keys, then gives me a second hug. "It was good seeing you."

She dashes to her car and peels out of the driveway. I sigh out of frustration, having let her slip away yet again.

"Yeah, they still love each other," says Mr. Davis.

"Any fool can see that," Todd adds.

"Well, the faster you two pack up my nice things, the faster he can come up with a plan on how to wear my youngin' down." Mrs. Davis giggles as she pats my arm on her way upstairs. "Whew! I tell ya, Todd, when you and Landon said the house down there didn't have stairs, I was *sholl* hoping y'all closed that deal. My things are up here."

෴

The boys' night out gives me a sense of what Todd and his friends might be involved in. I judge them, but with an open mind, as they seem tight knit and trusting of each other.

The Jay character watches me closely when he thinks I'm not looking, then tests me once I've thrown back a few beers and shots.

"T, when you gonna put in a good word for me with Lil' Launa? Word on the street is ain't nobody keepin' our girl warm at night. Imagine that. She spent all winter cold in that big house. Before you know it, it's gon' be cold as a motherfucker again in the blink of an eye."

"That might not be the case for long," says Todd.

"Why you say?"

Todd looks at me.

Jay grins. "I knew you ain't bring this man around for nothin'. So what you sayin'? He family?"

"*Tryna* be."

Jay extends his hand to me. "I respect that. I've been tryna crack that one for some time now, but ol' T here been blockin' me since day one. Good luck, man."

I scowl as I extend my hand. "I can't bring myself to say thanks to that, but I appreciate the free drinks tonight."

His eyes narrow at me. "It's a long drive back to Flint. Y'all need me to comp y'all a room at the hotel?"

Todd laughs. "Who are you hitting now, man?"

"You let me worry about that."

The two of them chortle as I'm left out of the loop. While they cackle and share inside jokes, I make my way out to the car. When Todd finally joins me, I sense he misses his old life from the look of nostalgia written on his face.

"You ready?" he asks me, turning over the engine.

I rub my hands together and sigh deep. "As I'll ever be."

Chapter 19

Leos

Launa

Todd drives off when I answer the door. Levi stands at my threshold, tall and handsome, exuding sexiness I can no longer deny.

I welcome him inside without hesitation, and we stare at each other in the dark. The buttons on his shirt shine from a low light coming from the moon slipping between the drapes. I count them, remembering what his chest looks like behind them.

"You stopped writing."

"What I have to say doesn't belong on paper," he says.

"I enjoyed reading your letters."

"I'm glad to hear it. I have to admit, writing them was therapeutic, and seeing you today has healed me further. I miss you, Launa."

I don't have to hear any more words from him. I jump in his arms, and sparks immediately fly. Through heavy breathing and passionate kisses, we strip each other's clothes off, ignoring a conversation that needs to be had.

The taste of his skin in my mouth makes me feel like a giant, even though he is towering over me. He sighs so loudly my ego boosts. He's enjoying my lip service, and I get more excited as he sounds off his delight.

He pulls my mouth off him and lifts me against the wall. My leg rests in the crease of his arm, and the other slides across his shoulder. His fingers intrude my pussy, then return to my mouth. I suck them slowly, looking into his eyes.

"Now let me taste you," he says.

His strength captivates me as I'm lifted up the wall and held sturdy and safe above his submerged head feeding from my cup. I trust he won't let me fall. I trust he won't sample me for long because my throbbing walls ache for him to fill me.

It's been too long since I have felt like this. So long that it suddenly hits me that Levi is a pleaser and will feed from me all night if he likes, while I suffer from impatience and yearning to feel his dick stretch my walls.

I moan, holding onto his head with flashing thoughts of our past encounters. Each time has been memorable, but in this moment, I am the happiest.

He lowers me and drapes my knees above his strong shoulders. I taste my essence when he kisses me, panting as his head slides between my drenched folds.

"Yes," I whine. "That's what I need."

"You miss me?" he asks, plunging into me strong and long.

"Yes, I miss you," I certify. "I'm sorry how I left you. I had to..."

He silences me with a kiss then moans, "Mmn un. Don't apologize. I understand everything and none of that matters." His slow rhythm transitions into a full-blast attack. "The only thing that matters is you." He strokes. "And me." He strokes deeper and holds his position with all of his prize inside of me. "In this moment." He exhales against my neck and pulls back. "Right now."

His thrusts surge through my pussy as my back thumps against the wall. Together, we slide up and down the sheetrock, moaning, groaning, and grunting from raw pleasure.

He pulls hair from the nape of my neck into a balled fist. "That's it. Drip it all on me," he says, drawing my juice. "You've been away from me too long, my love. Tell me I can come in you, baby."

"Yes," I reward him.

I want to feel his warmth met with mine. I want to feel him as long as I can. Live inside of me if he must.

I skirt out a shriek and look him in his eyes as he pours into me. His breath is cut short as he empties his load, pressing me between him and the wall.

I bite on his ear. "The bedroom is that way."

His body jerks and he carries me half-replenished and crashes in my arms with a smile on his face.

♡

I wake to the smell of coffee, classical music traveling to my room from the front of the house, and the bell ringing on the front door.

Levi shouts, "I got it!"

I scowl, thinking to myself, *'What the hell does he mean, he's got it?'*

Quickly, I freshen up and throw on my favorite lounge wear to be cute at breakfast.

"Who was at the door?" I ask him, walking into the kitchen.

"Them." He points to a penguin dressed waitstaff.

"You mind telling me what these people are doing in my house?"

He pulls out my chair at the table. "Have a seat."

The staff showers me with pink rose petals like a stripper being thrown one-dollar bills, while Levi signals for a live violinist centered amongst them to change the song.

The violin strings belt out a classical rendition of *"What Do the Lonely Do at Christmas?"*, the song we danced to at the hotel on our first date.

"Launa, it's been sixteen weeks and three days that I've tried to get over you. I can't. And that's probably because I don't want to. From the moment we met, I had a vision that we would be spending our birthdays together. And that vision will never fade. He takes a step forward. "I love you, Launa. And you said you love me, too. It's time we act like it." He waves his hands between us. "*We.*"

My hand shifts to hold my heart in place.

"I chose pink flowers to shower your feet because they remind me of the gloss you wore on your lips when we shared our first kiss. Do you recognize the song the violinist is playing right now?"

I nod with tears welling in my eyes.

"The lyrics in that song describe me without you. I'll be without jolly for all four seasons if I don't have you at my side. That's where you belong, Launa. By my side. Seeing the world together." He closes in on me and lowers down to one knee. "Launa Davis, I want to share what's left of this lonely life with you. A breeze carried me in your direction the day I saw you, like it knew you were the breath of fresh air I desperately needed. Help me breathe again and say you'll be my wife. Will you marry me?"

"Yes. Yes. I will marry you." I lean down and welcome his lips to kiss mine.

The lips I've missed for too long, and I hold onto them for as long as he lets me.

Chapter 20

My Gift To You

Levi

SECURITY IS TIGHTER ON SHARPER SR.'S estate than a presidential debate for our Winter Wonderland Wedding. Being wed on Christmas Eve grants us a small, intimate ceremony with close family and friends, and doesn't warrant this much attention, but I'm confident, if anything, the wedding will go as planned.

White string lights brighten the snow covered grounds as the darkening sky shares a rising moon and falling sun. Flakes of snow drift from imported white blossom trees ornamenting the property, draped with ivory and blue hued lights that lead the way to a massive white tent behind the mansion.

Crystal chandeliers drape from the roof of the tent, cascading shades of purple and blue against a white marble floor. Frosted strands of pampas grass arch above the aisle and tie in the center, accompanied by white, blue, and purple string lights illuminating my bride's path.

Near the entrance, glass covered candles

line around the base of a pillar, shaped to form a huge L as the hostess welcomes the guests transported via carts from the front gate.

I watch most of them arrive from the main house. A light draft sends a chill through the heavy wooden doors when they open, cooling the heat of anticipation overwhelming me. As the invited take their seats below the heated tent dressed in ball gowns and black tie, I shake my head at the grandeur of our special day, and can't thank Nadia enough for planning it.

I skim the crowd mingling in the cushioned seats covered in white linen. Each row holds three couples, sectioned off by white roses threaded at the top of each chair. The music of a harpist strums classical renditions of top-40 hits, entertaining the guests until Nadia calls for me to take my place center stage before Launa graces us with her presence.

"Nadia outdid herself with these decorations," I say to Maximus, standing as my best man.

He hums a laugh. "She had help from Olive. Remember her? Tall, French model you hit on after the divorce when you were a bloke pipin' 'round?"

"Oh. Her. I saw her when the first few guests arrived. I wondered who invited her and did an about-face." I chuckle. "Now you're telling me I have to thank her?"

"Just thank Nadia. She wants all the credit." Mash snickers. "She's been talking about this wedding since you told us Launa said yes. Well done, mate."

The harpist stops playing a modern twist to a classical tune, and Nora Jones' voice croons from the speakers. Nadia sends the signal.

Mash pats my back. "It's time, loverboy."

I adjust my cufflinks and exhale a deep breath. "Yes, it is."

The gang from Charlotte whistles when I enter the tent with my mother and Mrs. Davis on my arms. I escort them to their seats in the front rows, then feed off my friend's energy and do a spin before taking my place below the decorated arch.

"I know that's right!" Shannon yells at me.

My eyes land on my mother, wiping her eyes before a black line runs down her face. I smile at her and my aunts on the verge of tears, then peer at my cousins staring at Shannon with schemes brewing amongst them. I shake my head at them on the sly. They pretend to respect my wish, but their slick grins tell me otherwise.

A collective shift in the room turns toward the aisle as Landon walks in with Mash. I crack up internally when Todd's smile disappears the closer they approach his row. He glares at Mash when they pass him until Landon looks back at him and smiles.

My eyes roam next to Todd where Jay sits with his son, Max. He laughs with me at Todd's jealousy. I give him a head nod in appreciation of him accepting the invitation I personally sent him.

Mash stands behind me and whispers, "We have to keep an eye on my father."

"Why do you say?"

"He's a menace around women. I saw him counting blue pills before I walked in."

"You're kidding."

"I wish. Launa's sister told me what he said to her, and I had to apologize for him."

We hide our snickers from the spectators.

"Let's pray he doesn't pop one until after the wedding."

I add, "And that no one pops a cap in his ass for being a line stepper."

Mash buries his face as we snicker. "That's my dad. The *habitual* line stepper."

Nadia positions my soon-to-be niece, Lila, at the beginning of the aisle. Low mumbles of adoration sound off as she tosses white roses down Launa's path. Her pale-blue dress sways as she bounces to the end where Todd is waiting for her. He kisses his baby girl, then sits her in his lap in the second row as the music changes to the bride's theme.

I stand tall and gather my hands to settle my nerves. My heart beats fast but steady as Launa steps inside our sanctuary. Her short veil covers her face, but I can see her smiling underneath, and it warms my heart.

Overcome with emotion, a trembling sensation rushes through my body. I grow anxious for her to complete her strut and stand beside me.

Mr. Davis gives me her hand and his permission to make her mine. I acknowledge my gratitude with a nod and hold Launa close to me with my hand wrapped around her waist.

"Patience, son," the pastor makes a joke. "We haven't gotten to that part yet."

Our guests share a light laugh at my eagerness. I lift Launa's veil and sneak a quick kiss. She puckers her mauve-painted lips, accepting my advance.

The pastor adds, "Well, it seems he's not the only one in a rush."

The laughs subside, and we begin the ceremony. Pastor Morris shares words of what it means to be a husband, with concurring hums and moans from the women in attendance.

"I didn't think you could be any prettier," I say to my bride.

"I've seen you get clean, but Mr. King, I can't wait to peel you out of this suit."

The pastor clears his throat. "I had a longer spiel to share with you folks about love, honor, and the respect of thyself, which carries over to the respect of your partner. But this bride and groom are ready to be joined as one." His voice lowers, and his brows raise. "Y'all can't hear what these two are saying up here, but I can."

Launa and I turn toward the guests and laugh with them. The pastor asks us to repeat after him and give honor to God. We vow as husband and wife to love, cherish, and respect one another, to have and hold each other from this day forward, to stand as one for better, and to forsake the worst of the world when it tests our union. We finish with a promise to never abandon our house over riches and struggles, and to remain a faithful house in sickness and in health until death parts us.

"I know the answer to this question, but Levi, do you take Launa as your wedded wife?"

"I do," I say, gazing into her eyes.

"Do you, Launa, take Levi as your wedded husband?"

"I do."

I kiss her before the pastor pronounces us as man and wife. An applause roars as I hold her lips with mine, feeling complete with my new wife in my arms.

"Do I have on any lipstick, husband?" Launa smiles, looking up at me.

"I swallowed it, I'm sure."

She raises her bouquet as we walk up the aisle to cheers, whistles, and blown kisses. Nadia hugs us both when we exit and escorts us to a room on the first floor for us to have a moment alone and exhale.

"When I told you my family rotates the location where we spend Christmas, I never imagined it would be in London."

"They can thank you for that."

"And you." I kiss her lips. "How are you feeling?"

"A little jittery, but I'm good. How about you?"

"Excited. Relieved. Happy. Anxious."

"Why anxious?"

"I have a wedding gift for you, and I'm ready to see your reaction."

"A wedding gift? Does it also count as my Christmas gift?"

I laugh as I kiss her forehead. "No, my love. You'll have several to open in the morning."

"I better." She brushes her nose against mine. "I wasn't expecting a gift from you today, but I have one for you as well."

I kiss her bare shoulders. "I can't wait to see what you got me."

We join our family and friends in the open foyer for happy hour while the tent undergoes a transformation for the reception. It's big enough to be a hotel lobby. Regal décor covers the mansion from wall to wall as if a royal lives there. In its own way, one does.

How Nadia convinced her father-in-law to host our union on his estate puzzles Launa and myself, but we're eternally grateful as the place is making our day more memorable than we could have imagined.

A waitstaff serves hors d'oeuvres and champagne, and security surrounds us as we're photographed inside the home. It would be intense if love wasn't flowing freely amongst us with laughs from our friends and family keeping the mood light.

My grandfather shakes my hand and pats my shoulder. "Can't count your grandmother out even in the afterlife. Can you boy?"

"I'd like to think she sent Launa my way."

"She'd be in tears right now if she could see how happy you are. I'm proud of you, young King."

Launa and I are the last to leave the main house. We return to the tent hand in hand as the Kings, and perform a choreographed routine in the center of an ice frosted floor for our first dance.

Her father cuts in, and my mother joins me to complete the song, then Mash calls everyone to the dance floor as we wait for the food to be served.

"Everyone is going to leave here full tonight, so let's work up that appetite."

While the party is getting started, Nadia gathers Launa's circle of friends into the house.

"It's time for your gift," I tell Launa.

"Okay, give it to me."

"Follow me."

I lead her back inside the main house, and her mouth drops open. She looks at me and holds me so tight I can feel her racing heart beat through her gown.

"How?" she asks, staring at Jen and her son embraced in an emotional reunion. Her eyes fill with tears. "Did you do this?"

I wipe her face. "With their help." I point to Nadia, Maximus, and his father. "As you can tell from this estate, they are well connected—especially Senior. Apparently, when you're important or a celebrity, a broker can have guests board your private plane without verifying their identity. Nadia met Jen in Miami a long time ago. She did her makeup and remembered her face when we went to the building you found her in. Mash and his father arranged for her to leave Spain, and she's been living here, with his father under his protection. She's free, my love."

She leers at her friends fighting for a piece of Jen. "You may go down in history as the only person to bring Jay to tears." She points at him, waiting for his turn to hug Jen. "I was honestly surprised he came."

"It took some convincing, but both occasions were worth it."

"Levi, I couldn't love you more than I do right now."

"It's not a competition, but I think I've proved I love you more." I lift her chin. "If you want to take back whatever you got me, I'll give you another week to try and top my gift to you."

"I think we're even."

I chortle. "How is that even possible?"

"My gift has a no-return policy." She places my hand on her stomach. "That trip we took for our birthday was epic for many reasons."

She now has to wipe my eyes as I stand before her, feeling the most complete I've ever felt. I hold her in my arms as we stare at the contagious love spreading around us, relishing in the joy we both feel in this moment. But I attest my happiness outweighs hers, as she and our child are the greatest gifts I'll ever receive.

REVIEWS
ENCOURAGE
VORACIOUS
INTEREST
EVERY
WHERE TO
SUPPORT

ME, THE AUTHOR

I GREATLY APPRECIATE IT

An Affair Abroad
T.K. RICHARDS

A TASTE OF THE Forbidden
T.K. RICHARDS

Blend
T.K. RICHARDS

STRAIGHT LINE
T.K. RICHARDS

DERAILED
T.K. RICHARDS

THE CROSSING
T.K. RICHARDS

JUKE
T.K. RICHARDS

LOW COUNTRY LEGEND
T.K. RICHARDS

THE VAMPIRESS
T.K. RICHARDS

Still Just over YOU
T.K. RICHARDS

Mistletoe Mason
T.K. RICHARDS

EN ROUTE TO EMERY
T.K. RICHARDS

MY GIFT TO You
T.K. RICHARDS

T.K. RICHARDS
CAN'T QUIT You

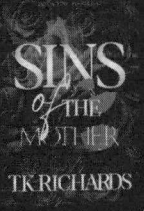
SINS OF THE MOTHER
T.K. RICHARDS

About the Author

T.K. RICHARDS is a multi-genre author of women's fiction and romance, featuring popular novels and novellas in Black Romance, Interracial/Multicultural Romance, Paranormal Romance, and YA Fiction. You can find her serialized fiction work on the Kindle Vella app. A graduate of Limestone University, T.K. has honors in Expository Writing, and was also the Poet Laureate of her graduating class. When she is not writing, she is immersed in the world of tennis, and binge watching movies—mostly comedy as she loves to laugh.

For more information about T.K. Richards, personalized orders, access to special deals, audio, character merchandise, and events, visit www.tkrichards.com and subscribe to my newsletter:

https://tkrichardsnewsletter.ck.page

You can follow T.K. RICHARDS on the platforms listed below to interact with her personally:

- facebook.com/Tkrichards
- x.com/tkrichards1
- instagram.com/t.k.richards
- tiktok.com/@tkrwrites
- youtube.com/tkrichards
- goodreads.com/T.k.richards
- bookbub.com/authors/t-k-richards
- amazon.com/author/Tkrichards